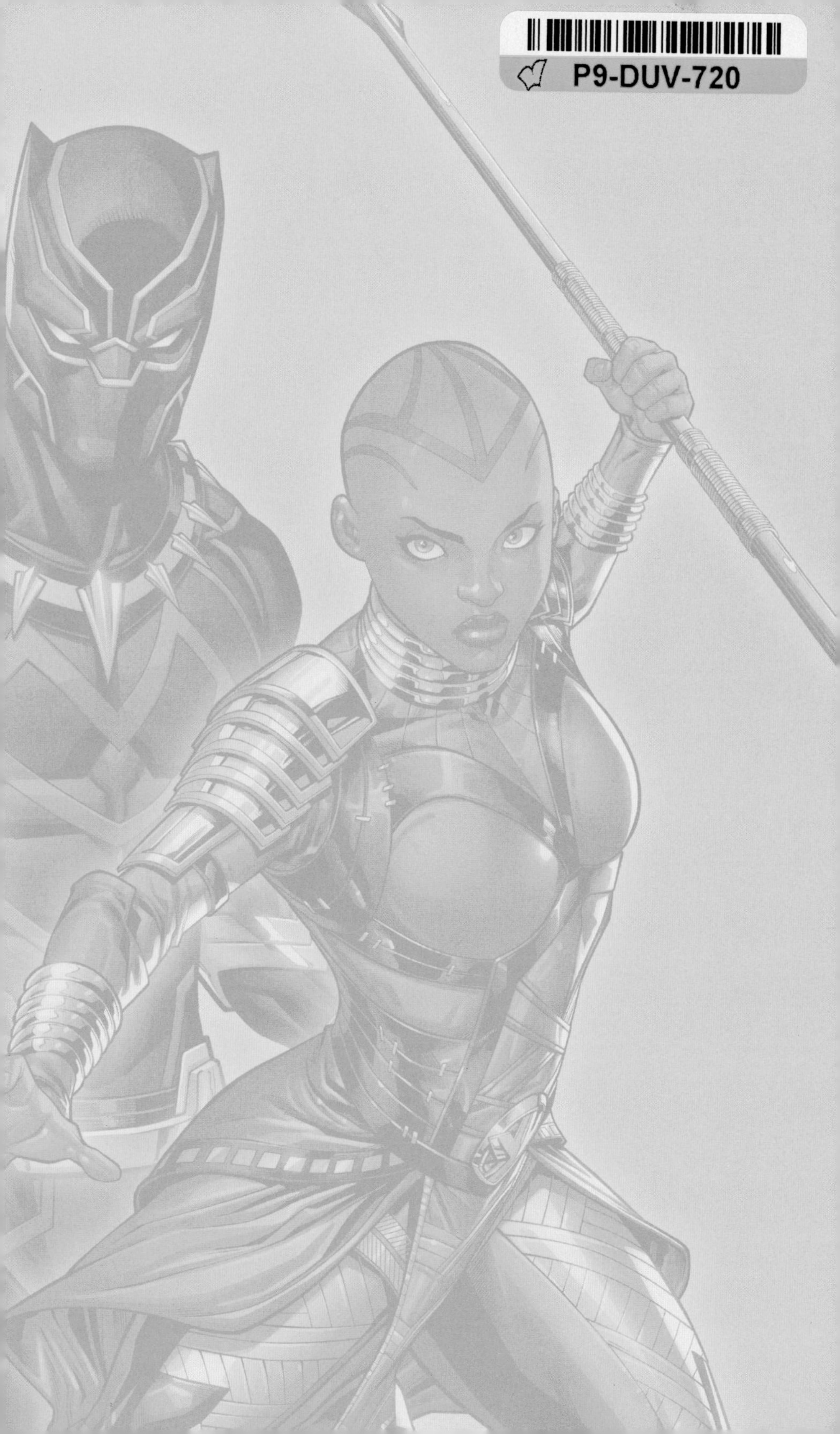

BLACK PANTHER

WAKANDA FOREVER!

Written by Julia March

Project Editors Pamela Afram, Matt Jones
Editorial Assistant Vicky Armstrong
Designers Stefan Georgiou, Thelma-Jane Robb
Senior Production Editor Marc Staples
Senior Production Controller Louise Daly
Managing Editor Sarah Harland
Managing Art Editor Vicky Short
Publisher Julie Ferris
Art Director Lisa Lanzarini
Publishing Director Mark Searle

First American Edition, 2021
Published in the United States by DK Publishing
1450 Broadway, Suite 801, New York, NY 10018

Page design copyright © 2021 Dorling Kindersley Limited
DK, a Division of Penguin Random House LLC
21 22 23 24 25 10 9 8 7 6 5 4 3 2
002–323469–Jan/2021

©2021 MARVEL

A catalog record for this book is available from the Library of Congress.

ISBN 978-0-7440-3712-8 (Paperback)
ISBN 978-0-7440-3713-5 (Hardcover)

DK books are available at special discounts when purchased in bulk
for sales promotions, premiums, fund-raising, or educational use.
For details, contact: DK Publishing Special Markets,
1450 Broadway, Suite 801, New York, NY 10018
SpecialSales@dk.com

Printed and bound in China

For the curious

www.dk.com

Contents

Welcome to Wakanda!

Wakanda is a small, wealthy country located in East Africa. The people of Wakanda treasure the ancient traditions of their land.

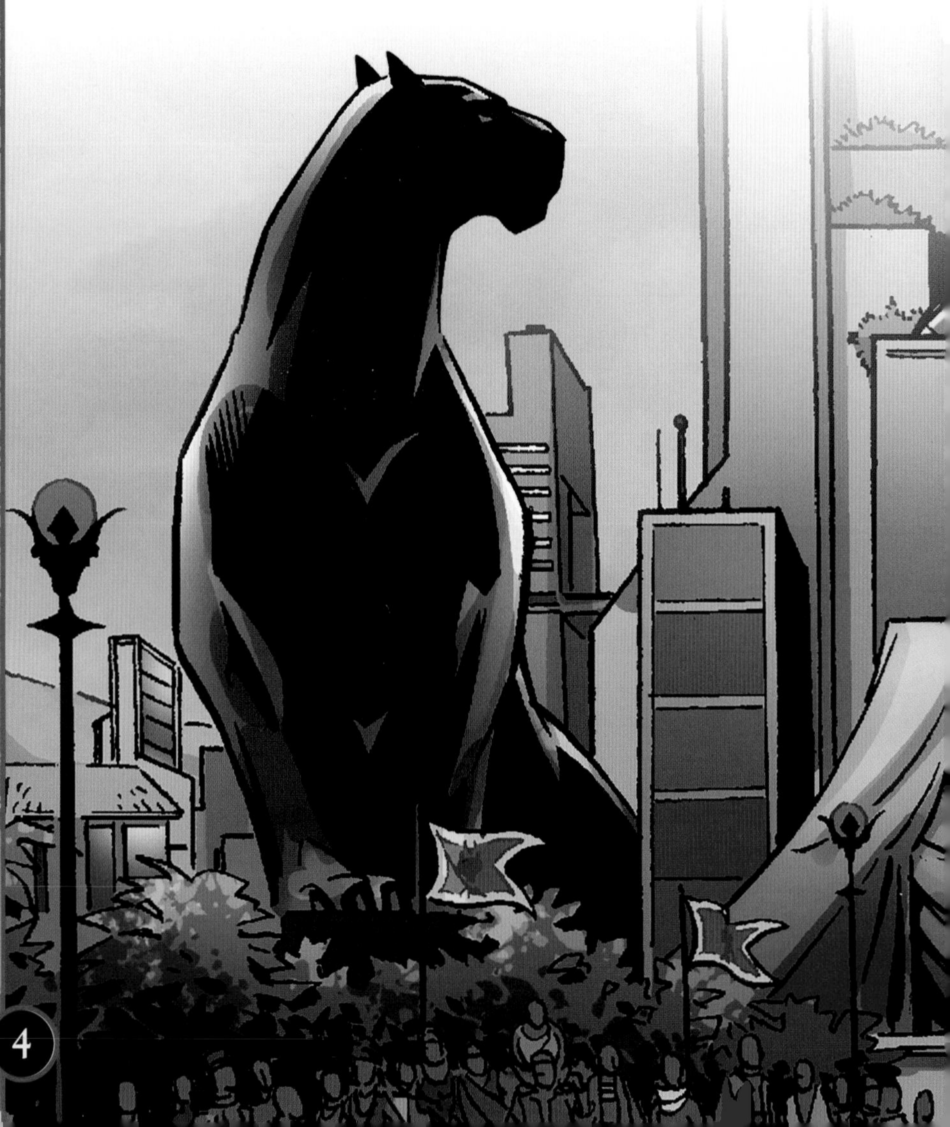

Wakanda has many secrets. Its people have developed incredible technology. Wakanda is a place like no other!

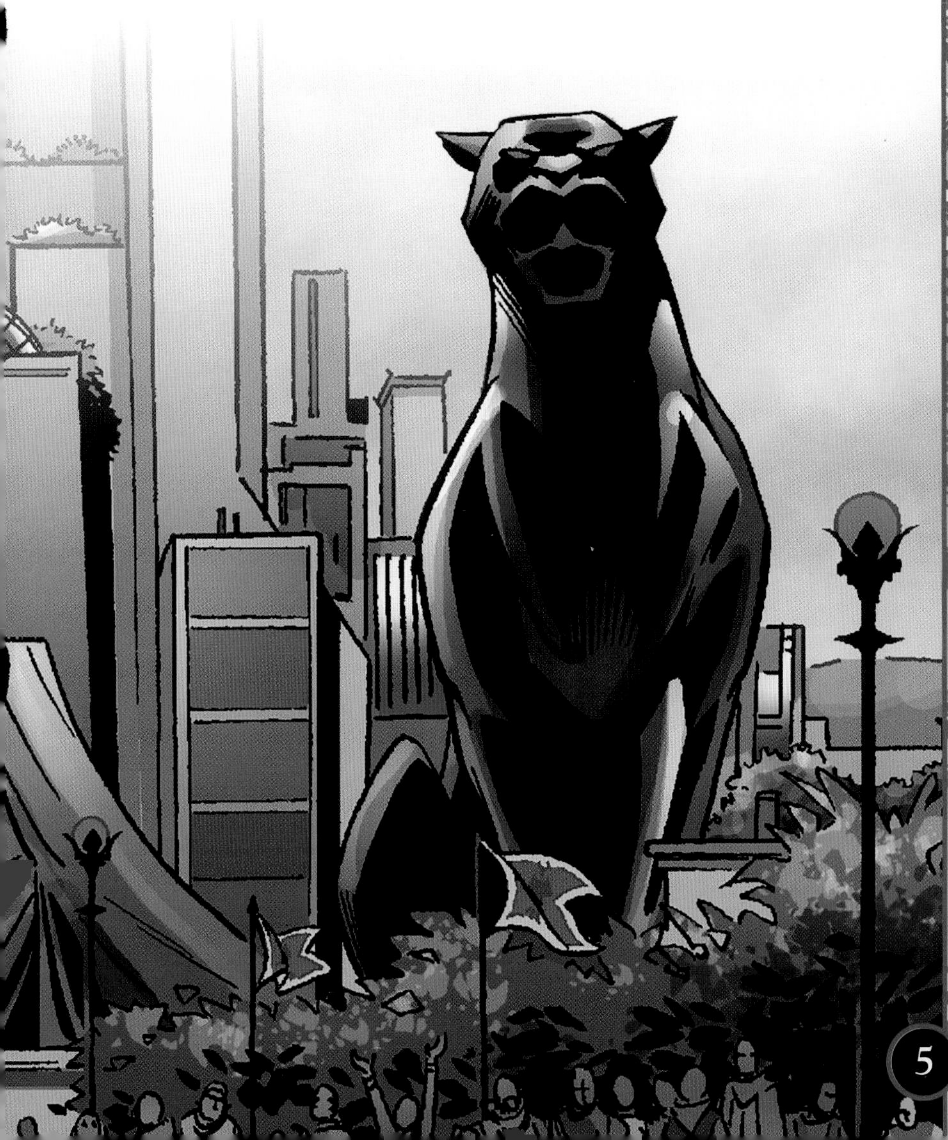

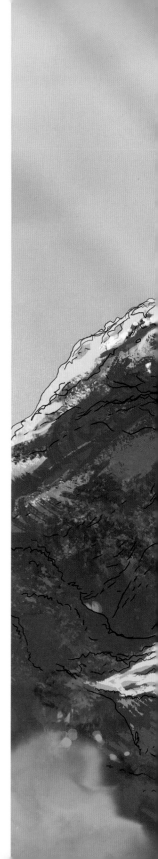

Wakanda's origins

One million years ago, a meteorite from space was discovered in land near Lake Nyanza in East Africa. The meteorite was made out of a metal called Vibranium. People settled on the land and called it Wakanda.

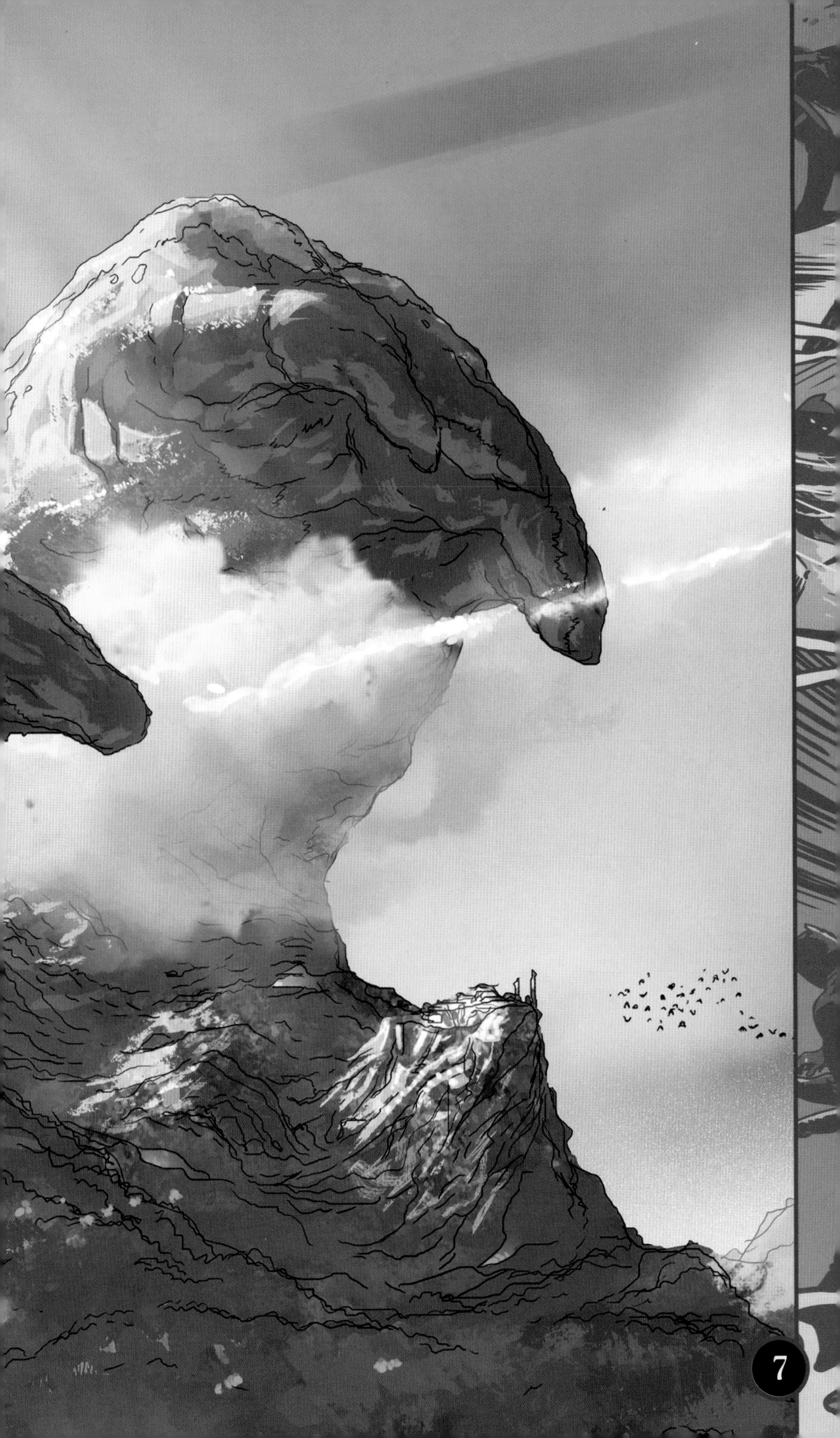

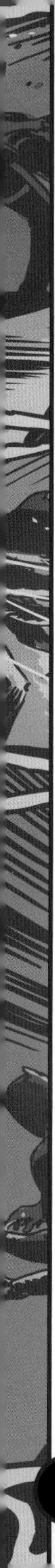

Meet Black Panther

Wakanda is ruled by kings or queens known as Black Panthers. The current Black Panther is named T'Challa. He is not just a king, but also a warrior and a scientist. T'Challa is also a Super Hero with incredible powers!

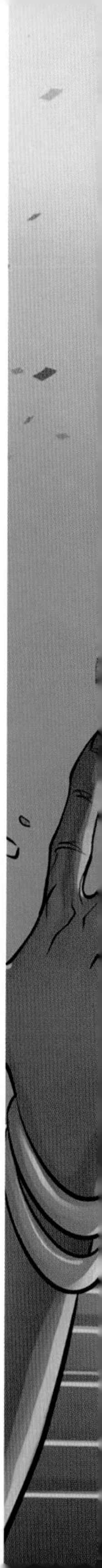

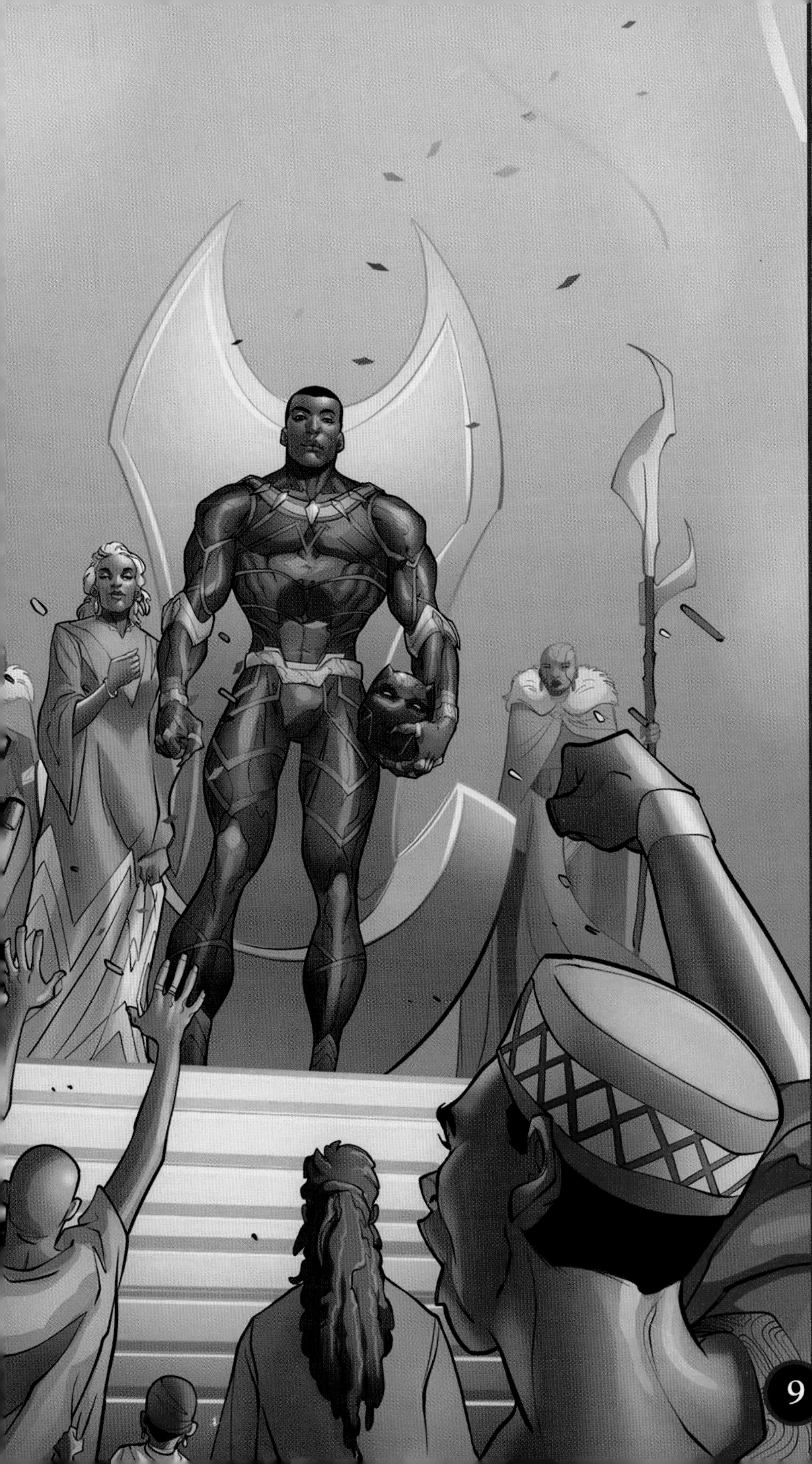

Technology in Wakanda

Vibranium is very important to Wakanda. Wakandans use Vibranium to develop amazing technology. They use it to make holograms and to fuel their vehicles. Wakanda keeps its Vibranium and technology hidden from the rest of the world.

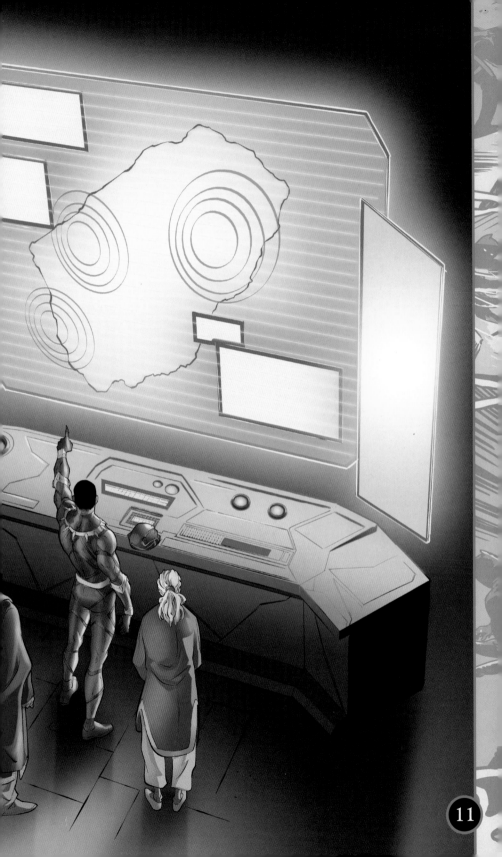

What does a Black Panther do?

A Black Panther protects Wakanda and its people from those who wish to do harm. This takes both battle skills and brain power!

T'Challa is very clever. He has studied science and combat. He is also skilled at using Wakanda's high-tech weapons and vehicles.

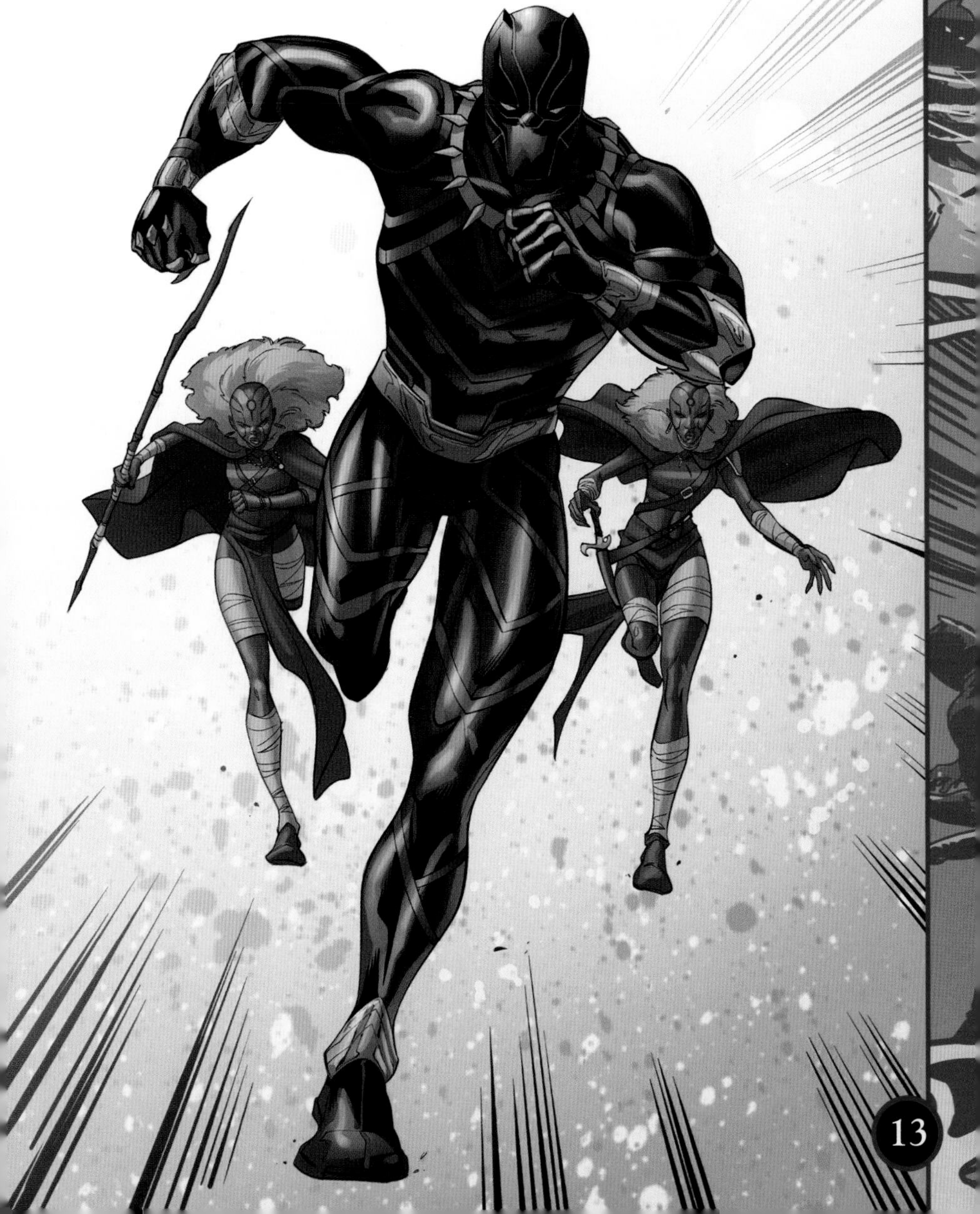

The Dora Milaje

A team of fearless female bodyguards protect Black Panther. They are called the Dora Milaje, which means 'Adored Ones.' The Dora Milaje are highly trained in combat and spying. They have taken a vow to protect Wakanda and whoever sits on its throne.

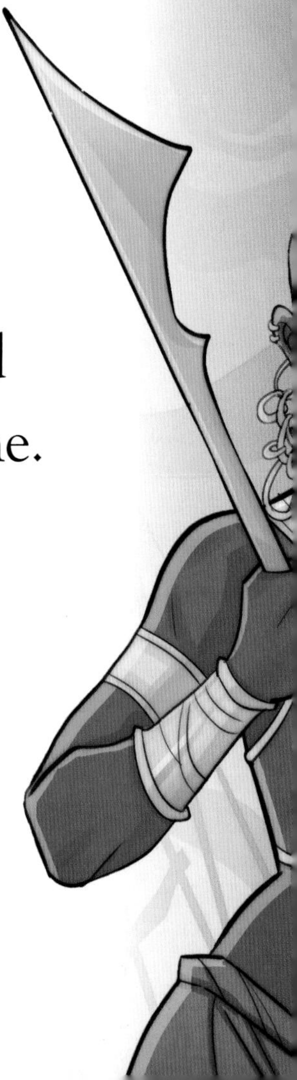

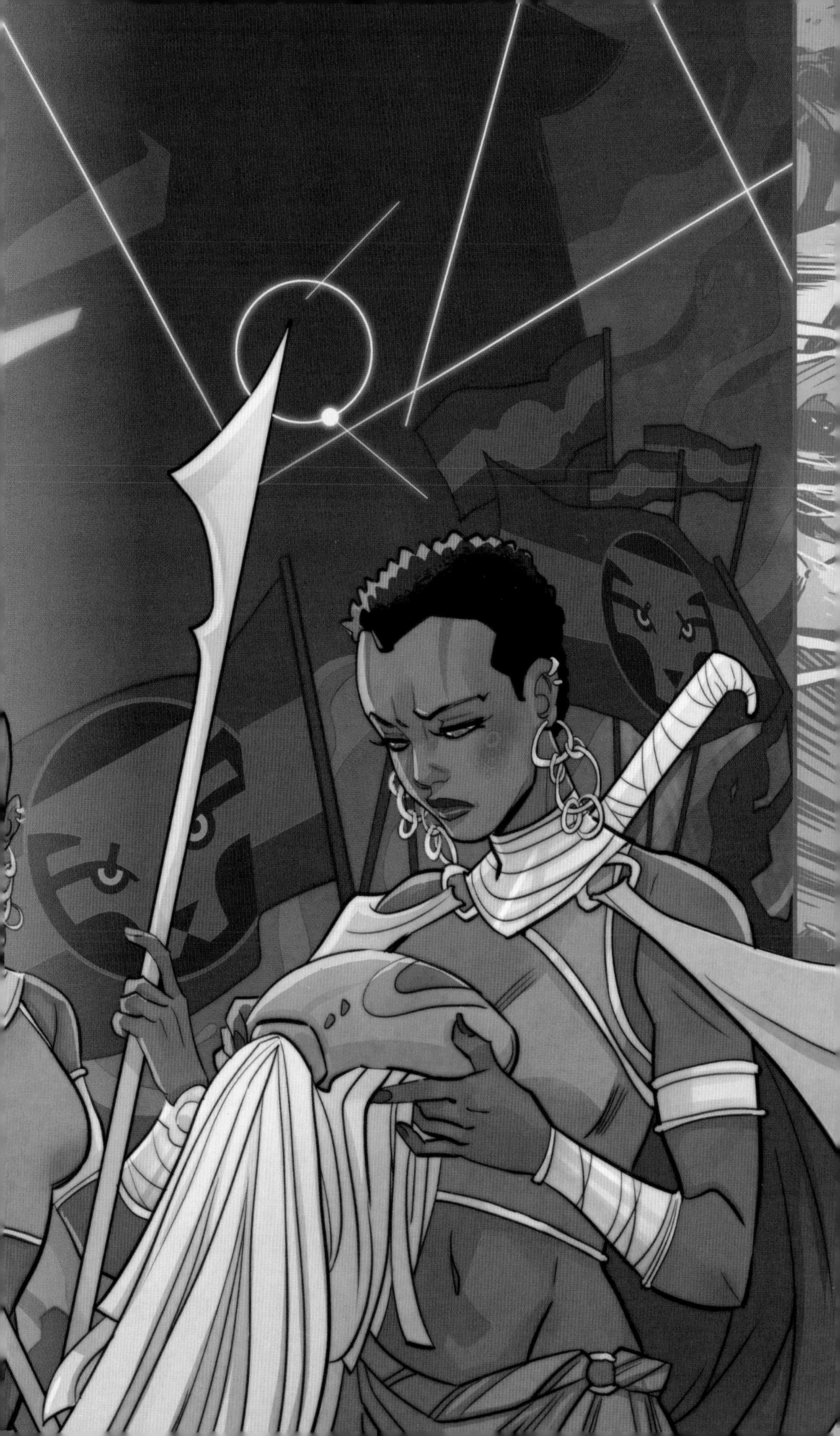

Shuri

T'Challa's younger sister is named Sh
She is one of Wakanda's finest inventors. Shuri designed Black Panther's Vibranium suit. She has also written special computer programs that can change people's brains!

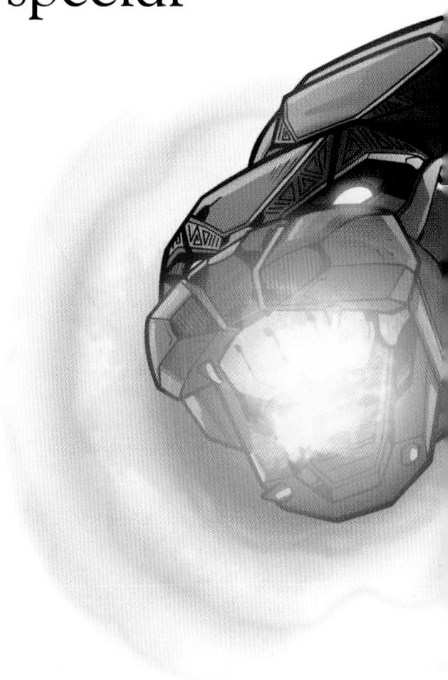

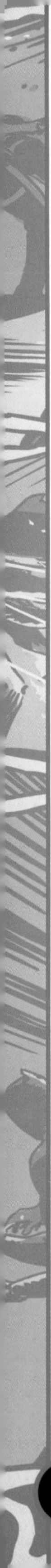

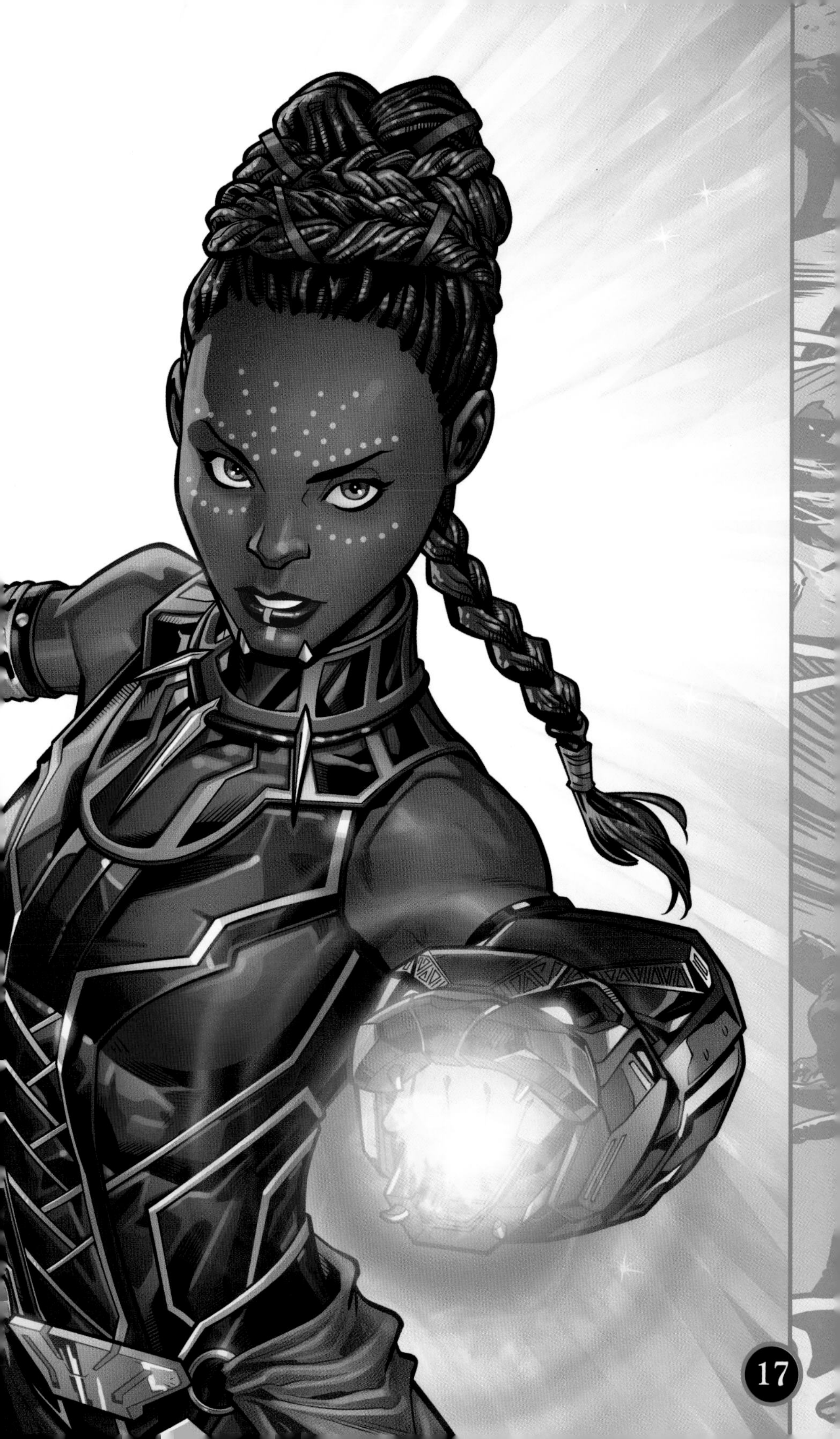

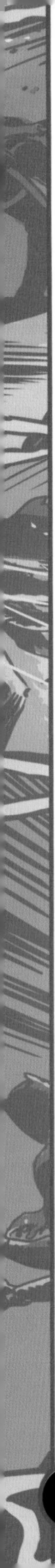

Brave warrior

Shuri is more than a talented inventor. She is also a brave and highly trained warrior, just like Black Panther. In fact, Shuri has taken over as Black Panther in the past when T'Challa could not do it.

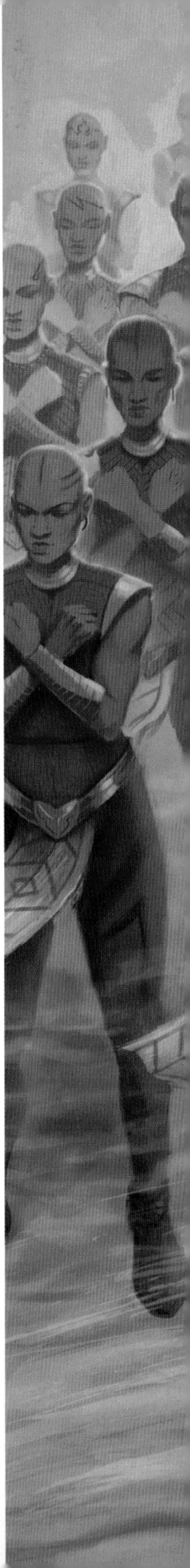

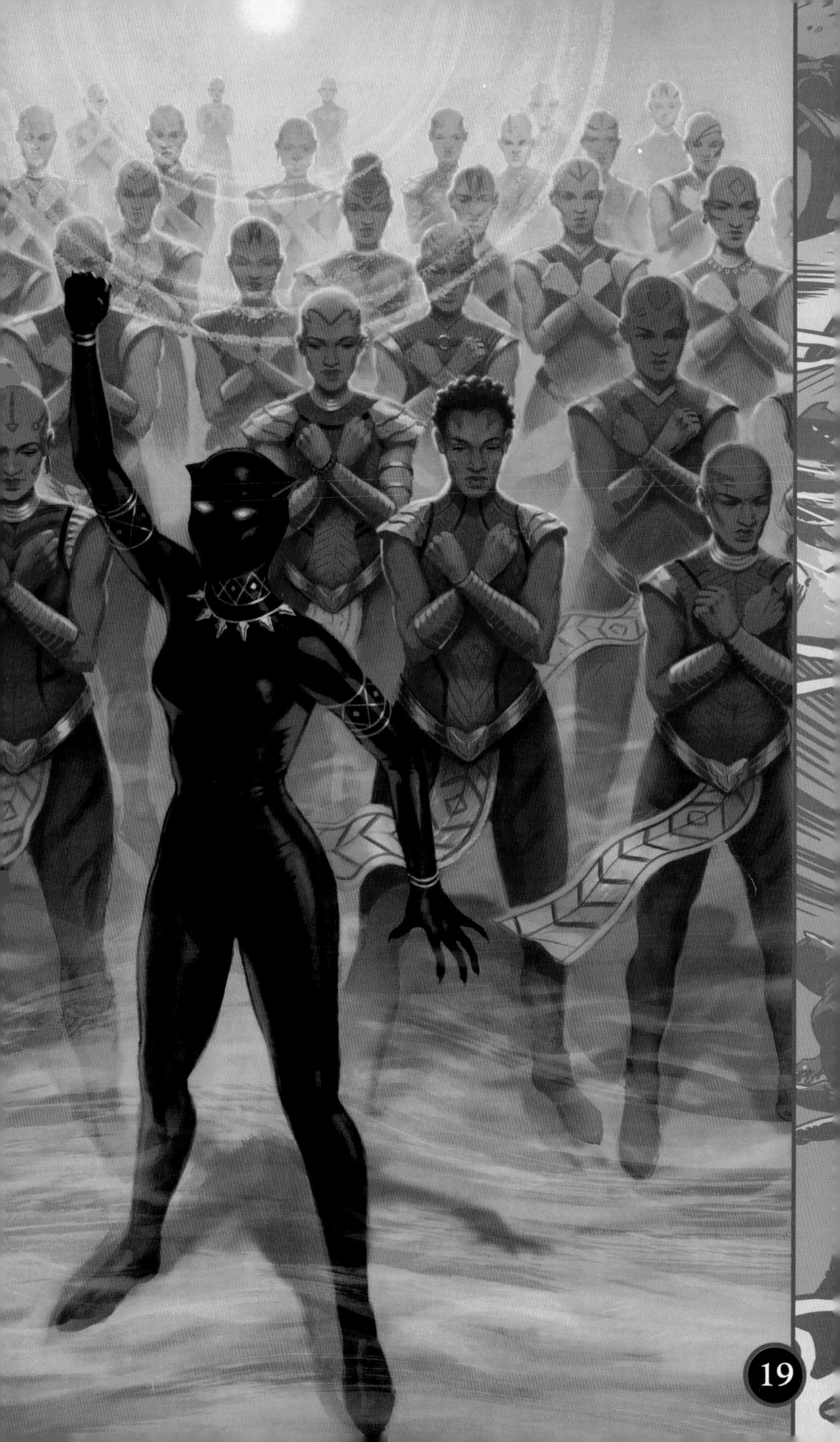

Panther Habit

Black Panther's special suit is called a Panther Habit. It is made with Vibranium, so it is incredibly strong.

Energized gloves increase strength

Vibranium in fabric absorbs energy

Vibranium boots help Black Panther to jump high

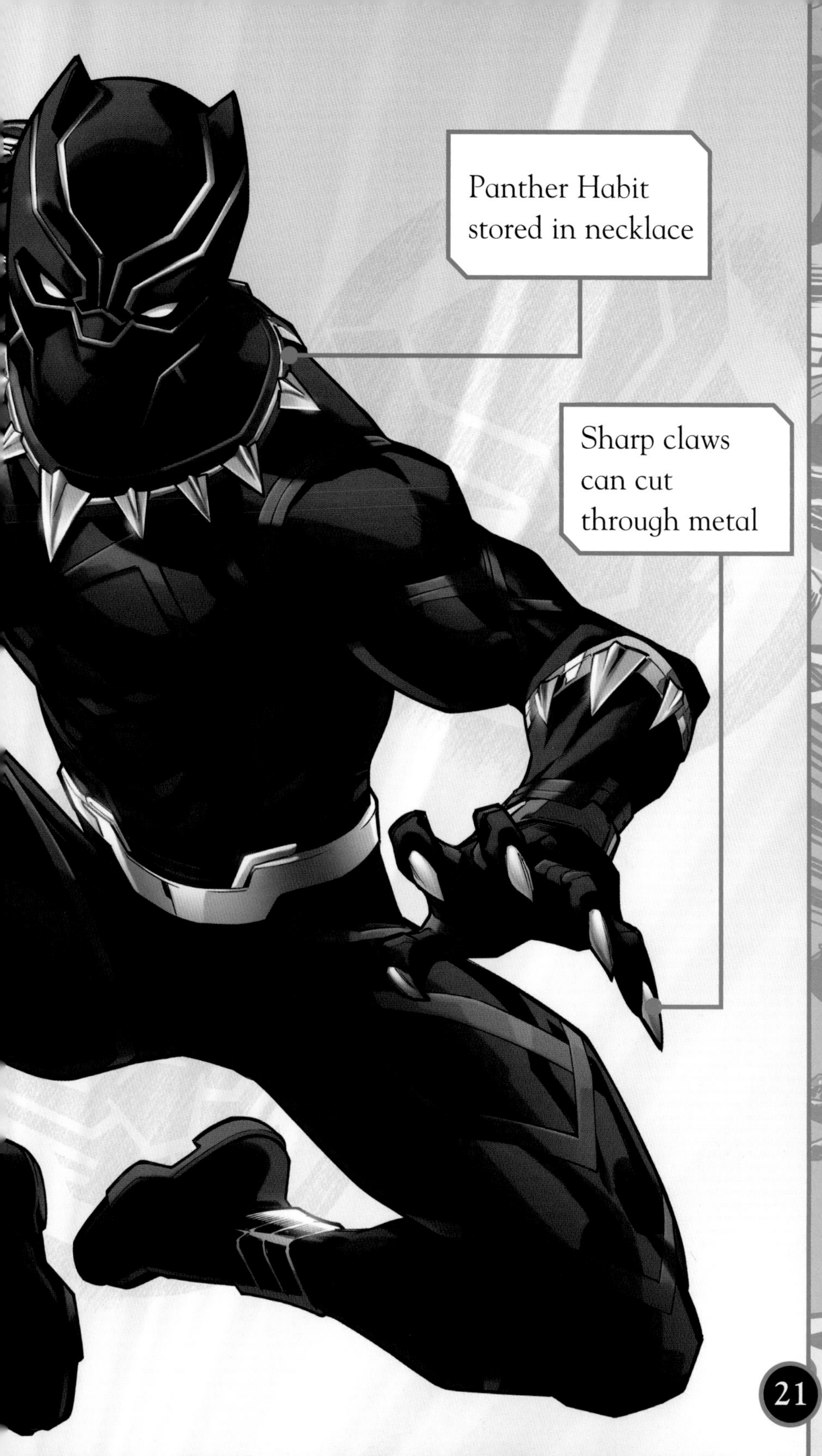
Panther Habit
stored in necklace
Sharp claws
can cut
through metal

T'Chaka

T'Challa's father was named T'Chaka. T'Chaka was the King of Wakanda and the Black Panther before T'Challa.

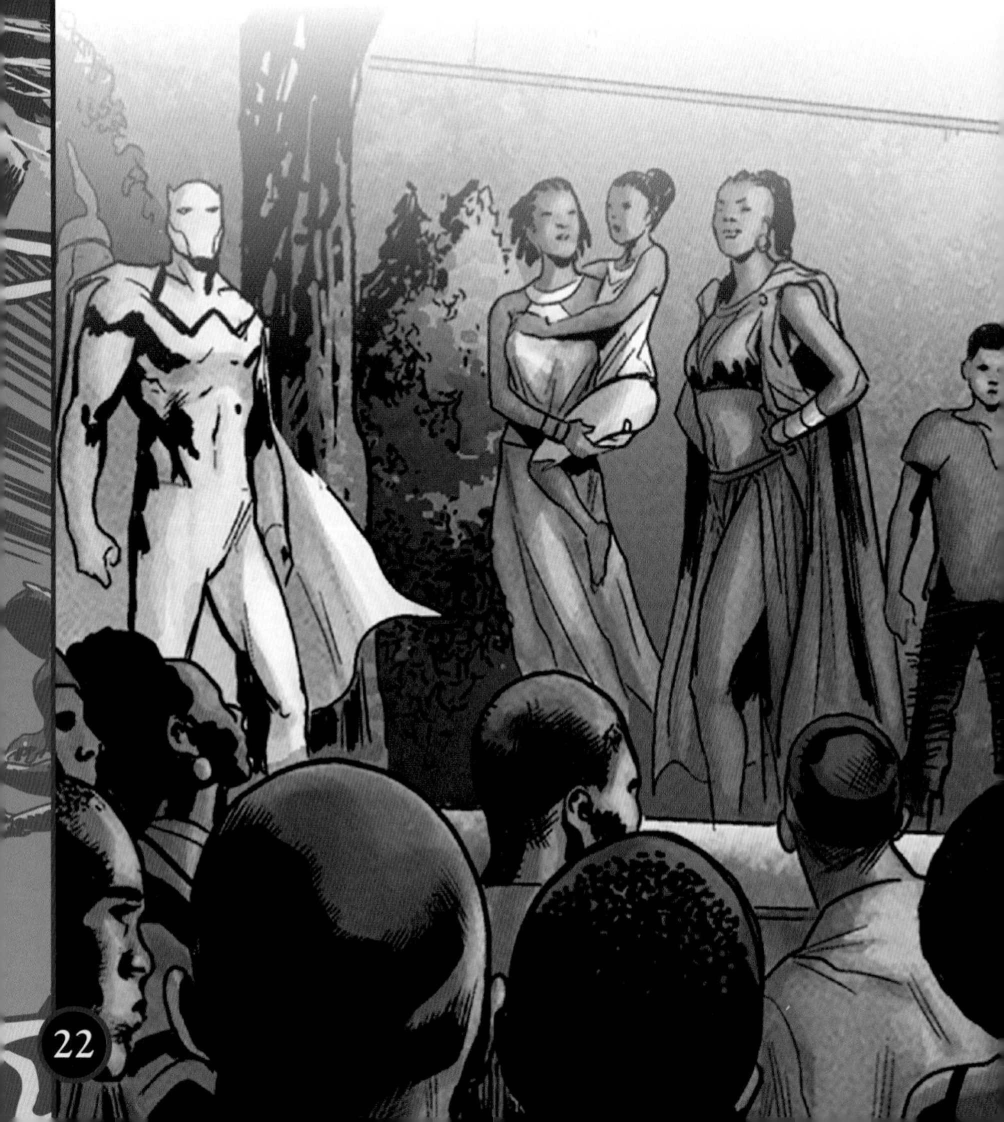

When T'Chaka ruled Wakanda, he focused on advancing its technology. He did everything he could to stop enemies from invading Wakanda.

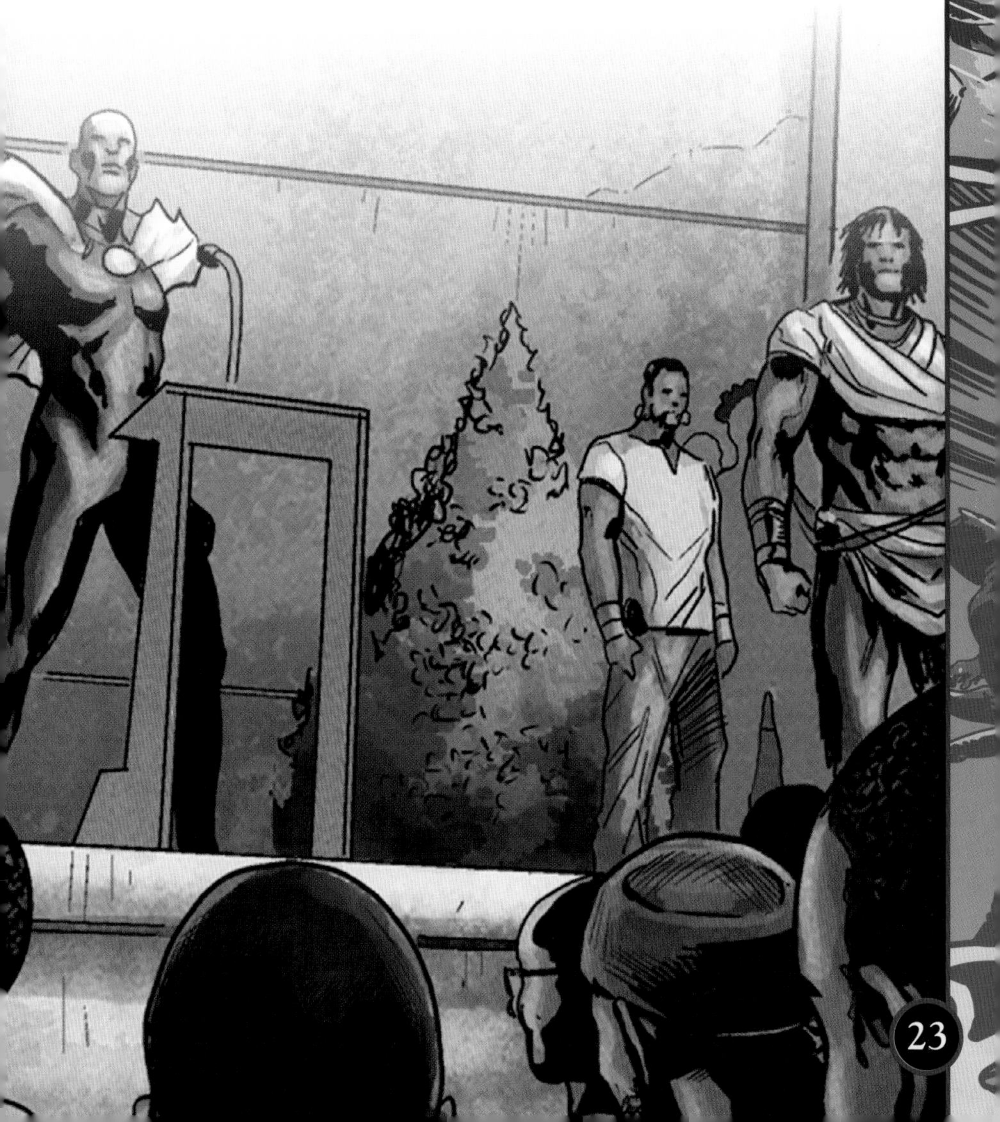

Wise Ramonda

Queen Mother Ramonda comes from South Africa, but she is fiercely loyal to Wakanda. She is Shuri's mother and T'Challa's stepmother. Ramonda shares a deep bond with her stepson. Black Panther always consults her before making important decisions.

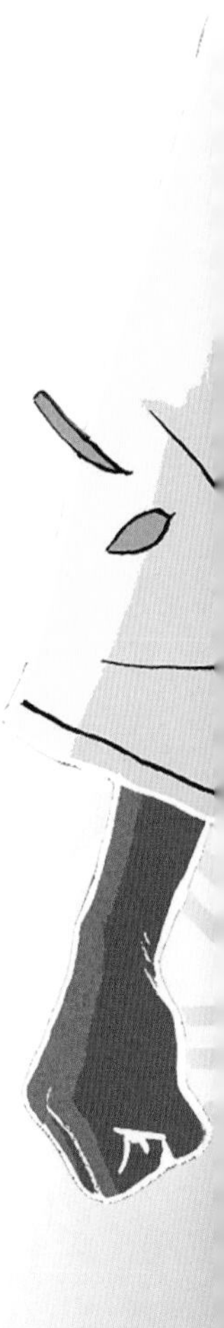

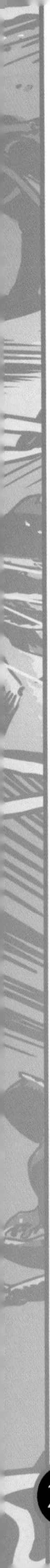

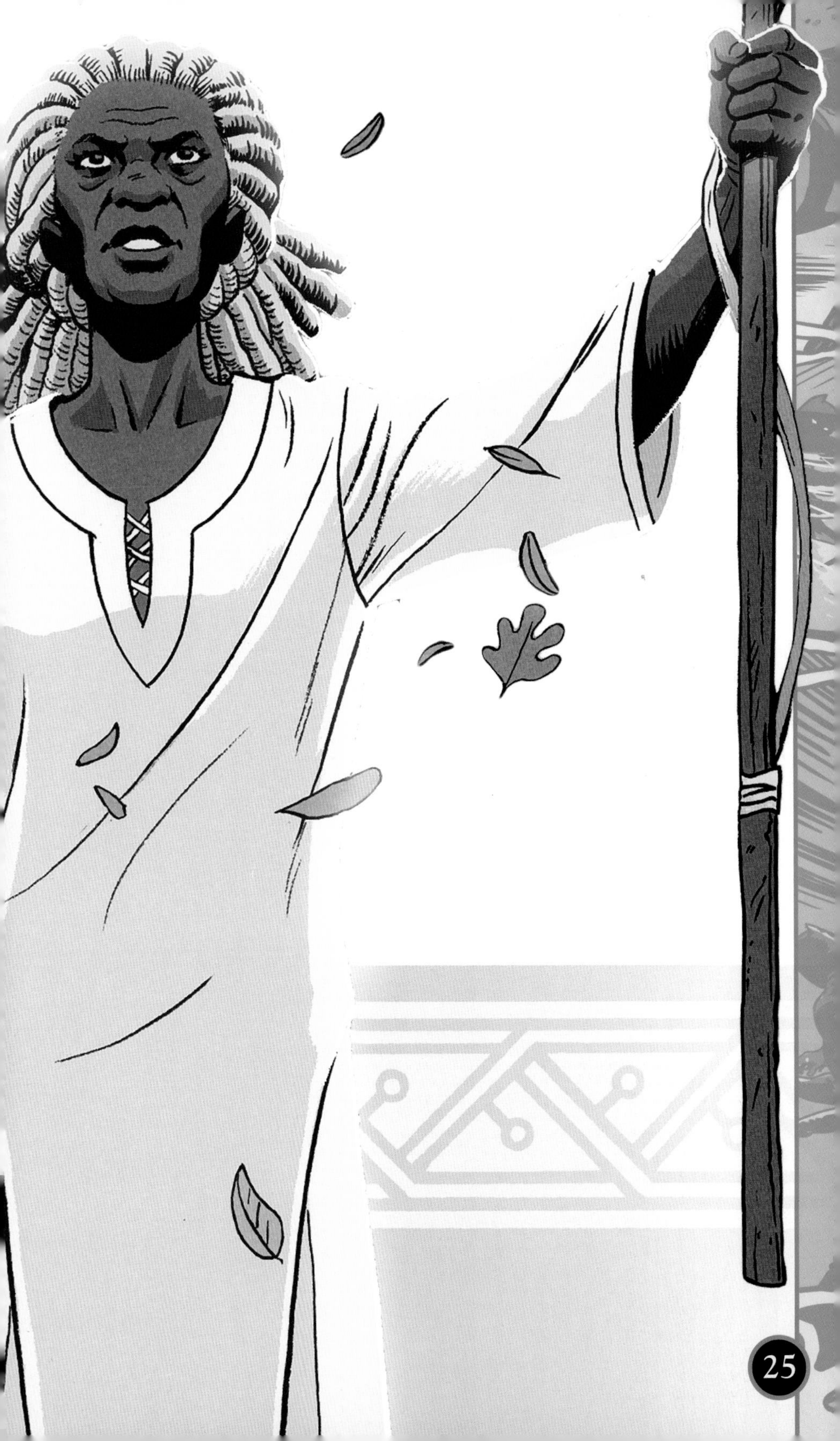

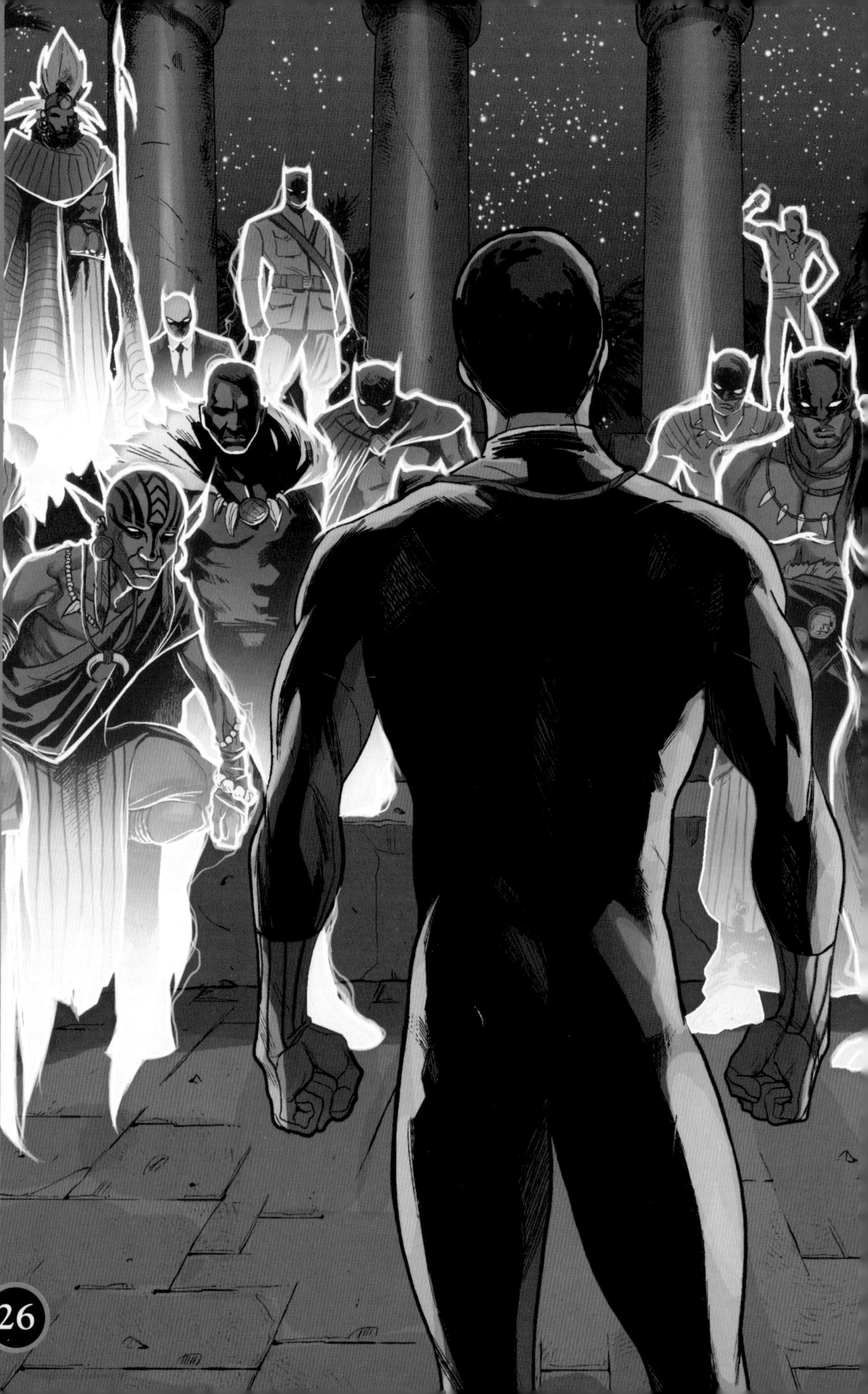

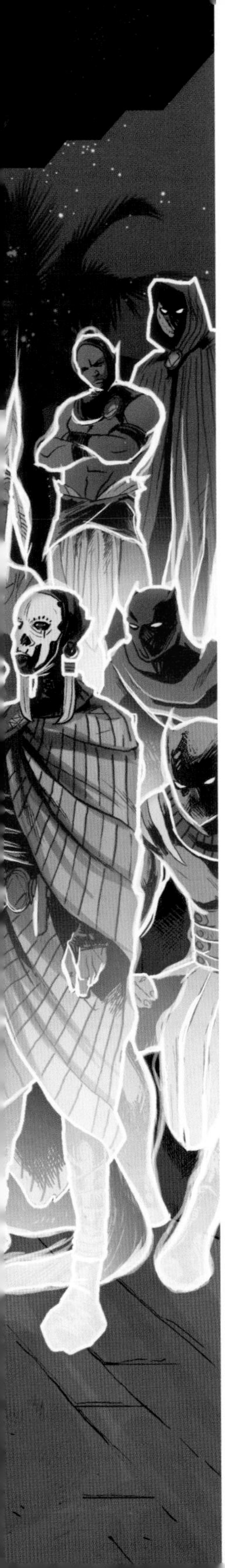

Protectors of Wakanda

Protecting Wakanda from its enemies is a tough job. Sometimes, T'Challa calls upon past Black Panthers to give him advice. He can even summon them to help him in battle.

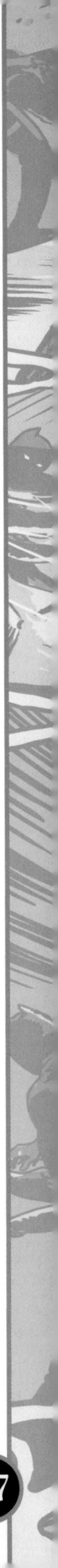

Vibranium

Wakanda is the only country that has Vibranium. It is a very powerful metal, because it absorbs energy.

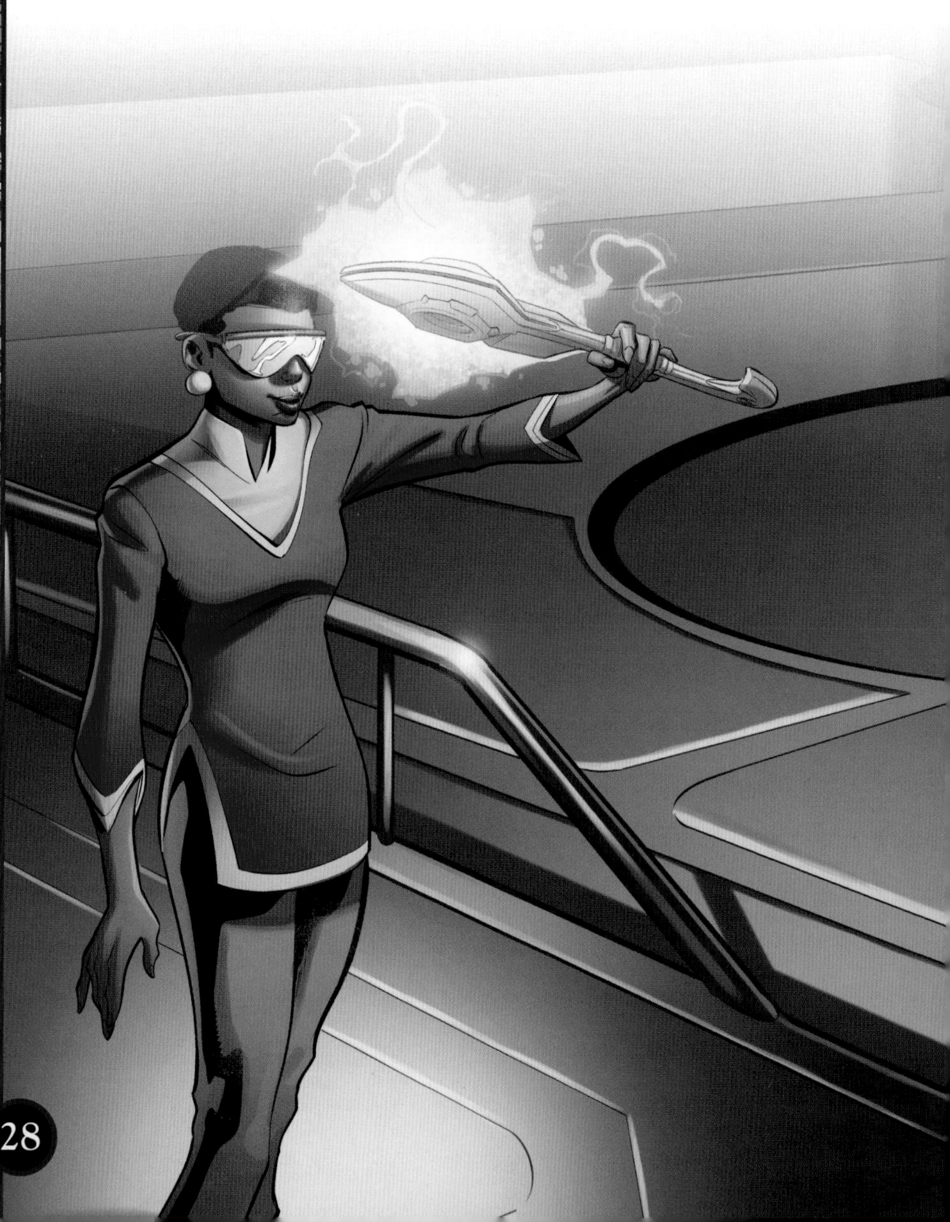

Very little can damage an object made of Vibranium. The metal is perfect for making armor, weapons, and vehicles.

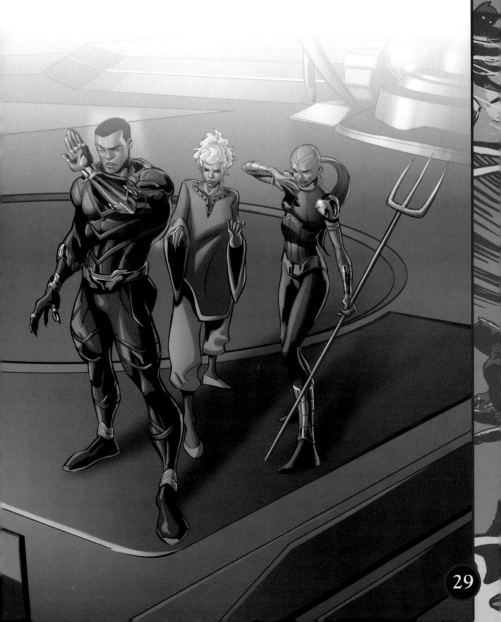

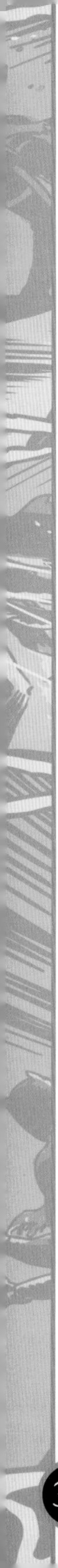

Panther potion

All Black Panthers drink a special potion to give them amazing speed and strength. The potion is made from a heart-shaped herb found only in Wakanda. The herb grows in Wakanda because of the Vibranium in the soil.

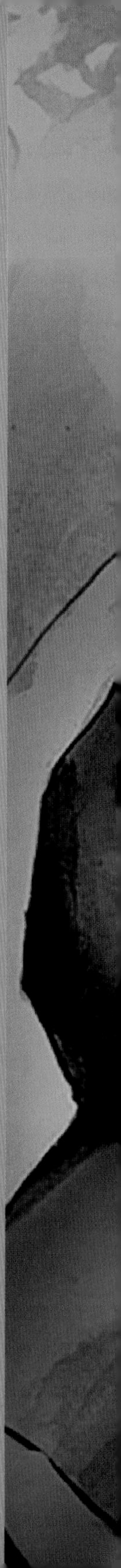

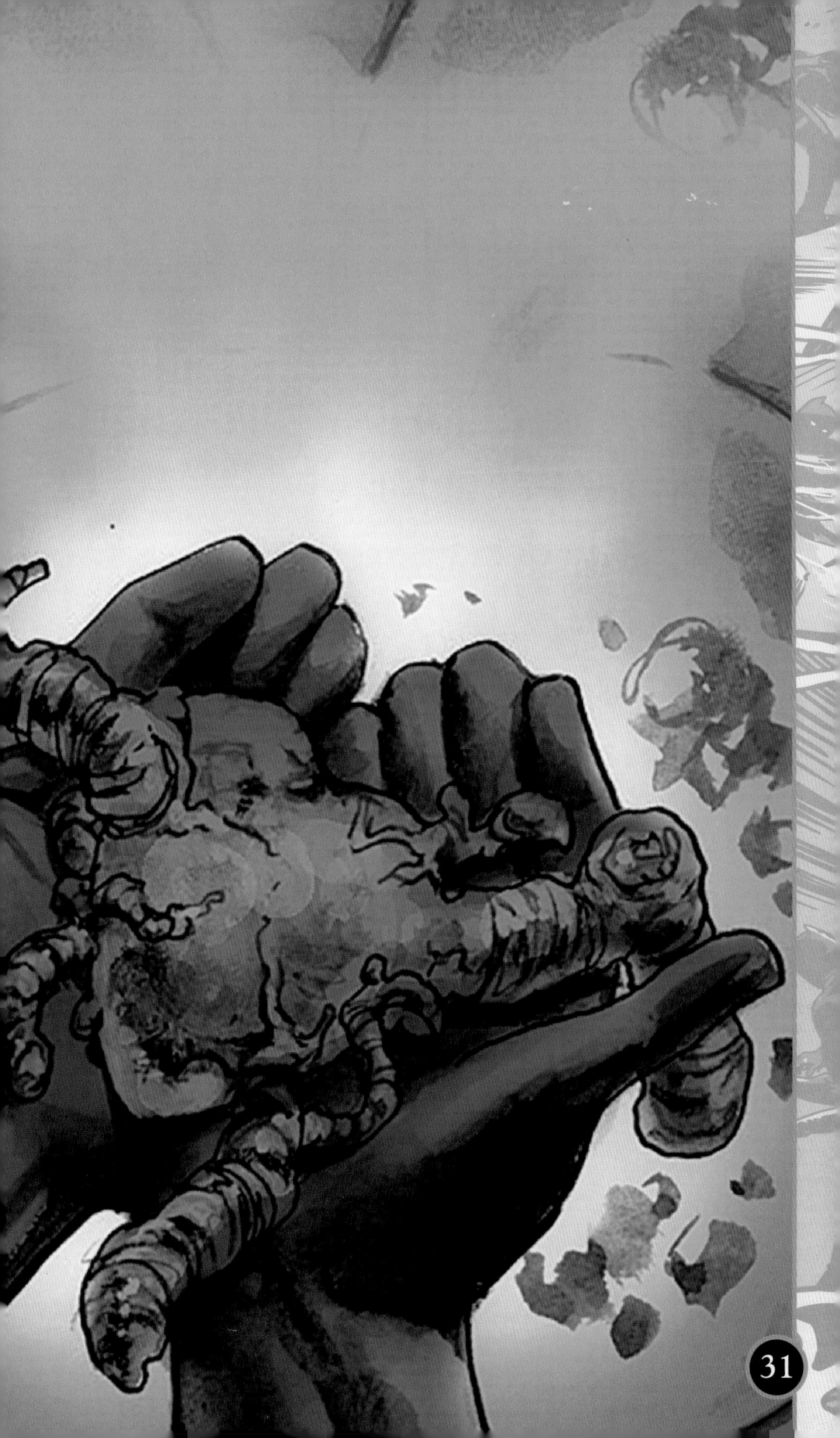

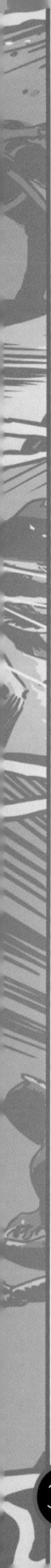

Wakanda and the world

For years, Wakandans have used technology to hide their country and its Vibranium from the rest of the world. T'Challa decides to reveal his country and its secrets. He wants to help make the planet a safer place.

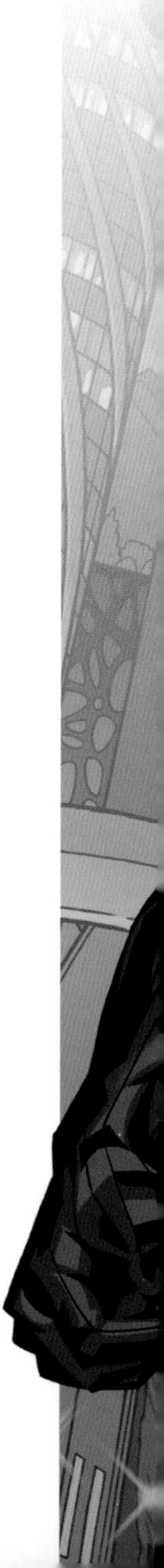

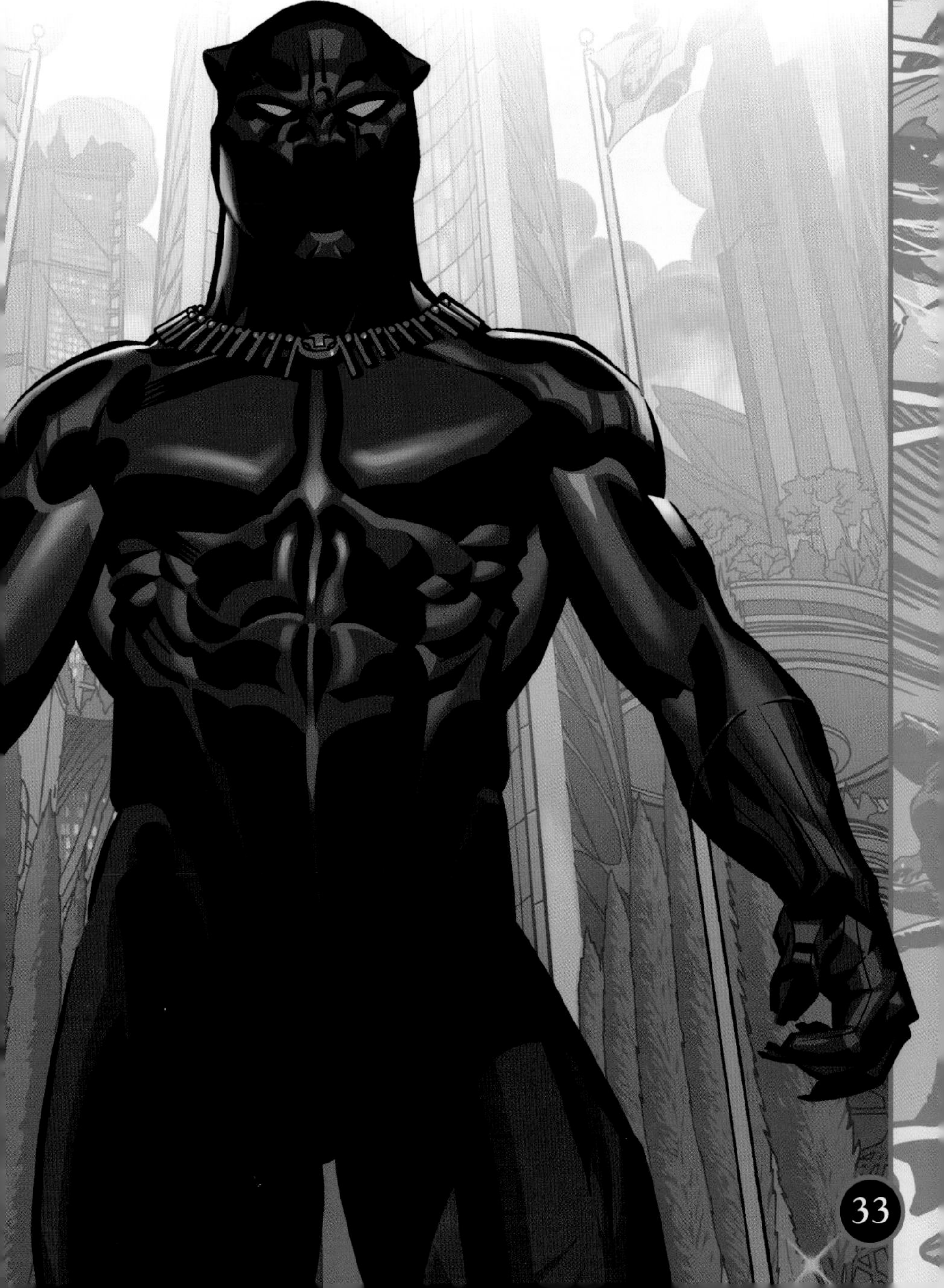

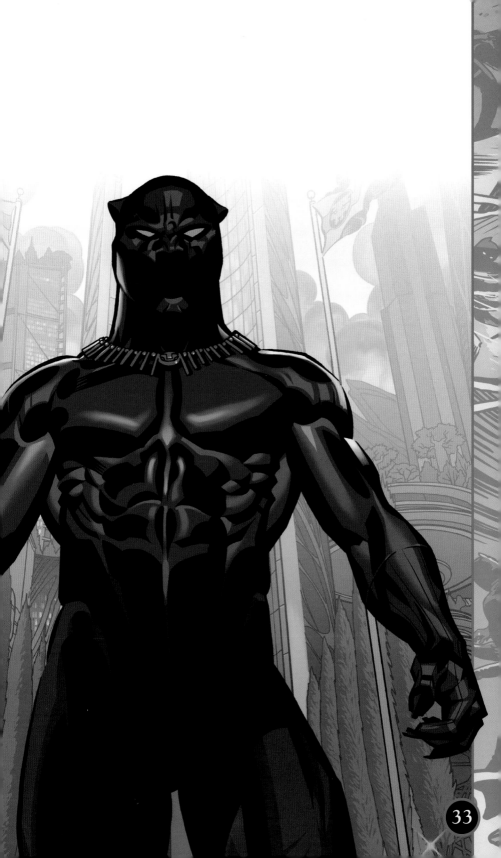

Okoye

Okoye is one of the most talented members of the Dora Milaje. Black Panther trusts Okoye. He consults her when planning missions. Okoye has traveled the world with Black Panther. She uses a Vibranium spear in battle.

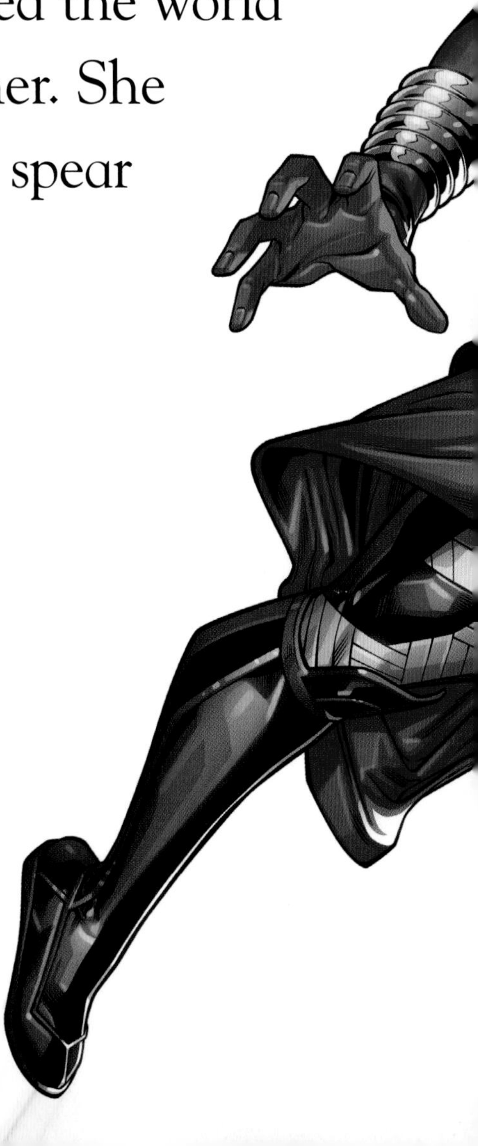

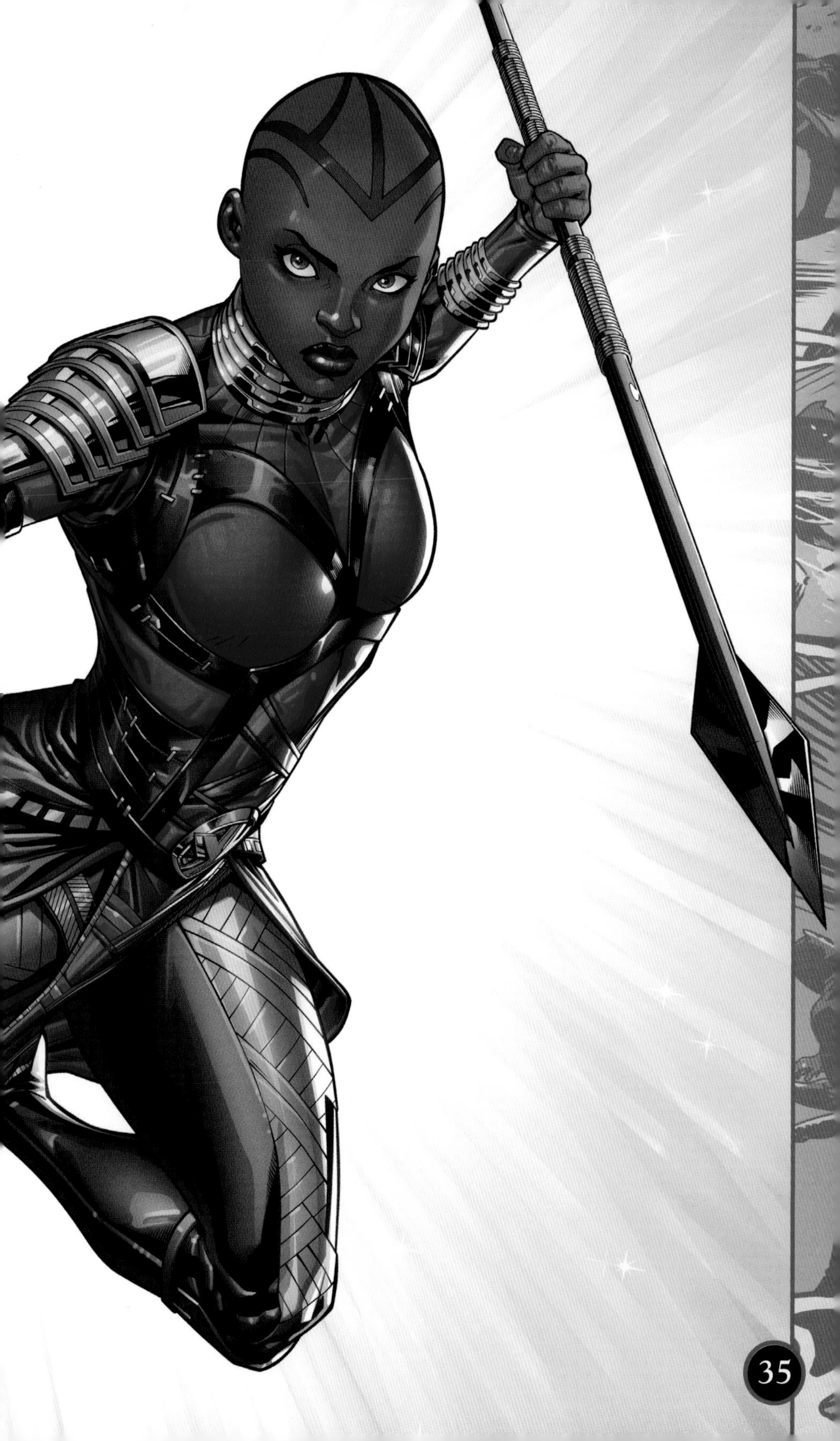

Avengers

Black Panther is the leader
of a Super Hero team named
the Avengers. He leads the fight
against evil all over the world.

Captain America is one
of the bravest Avengers.

Black Widow is the
Avengers' best spy.

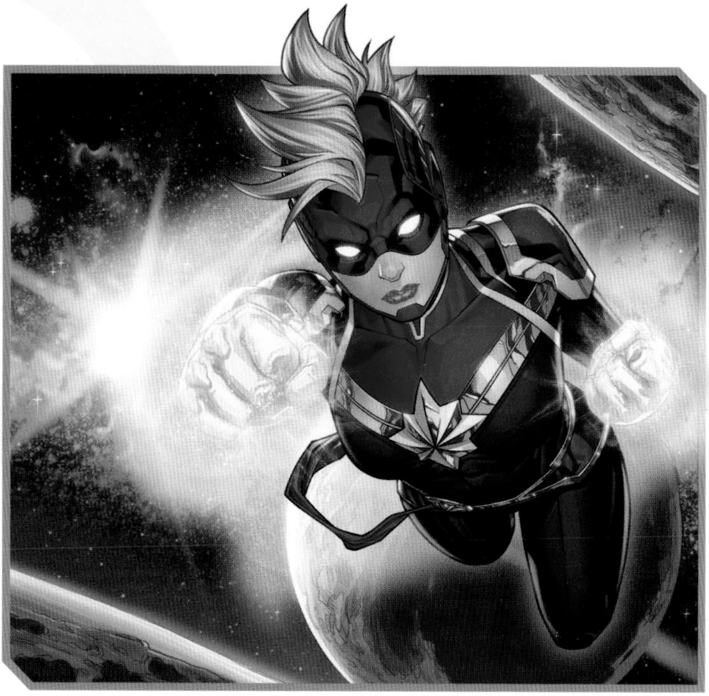

Captain Marvel
can fly in space.

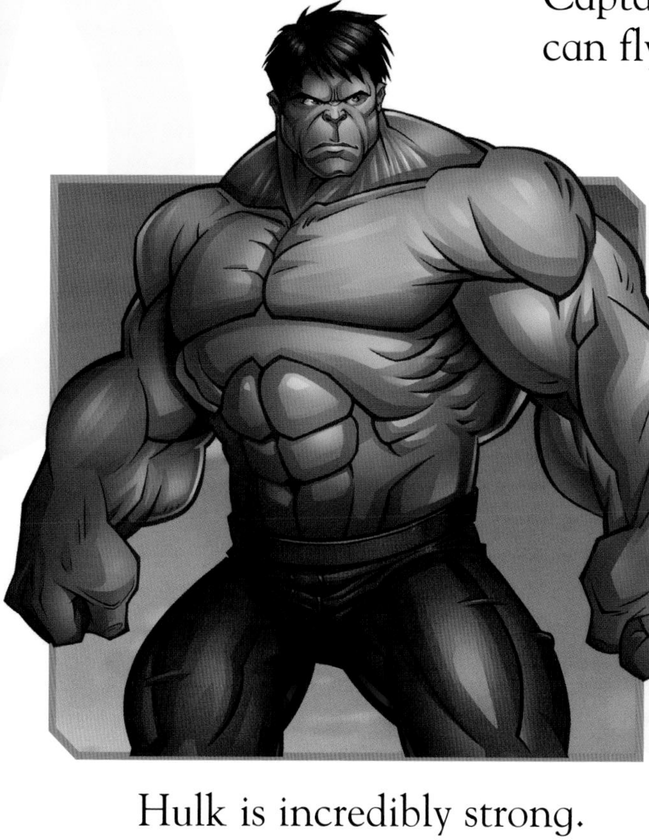

Hulk is incredibly strong.

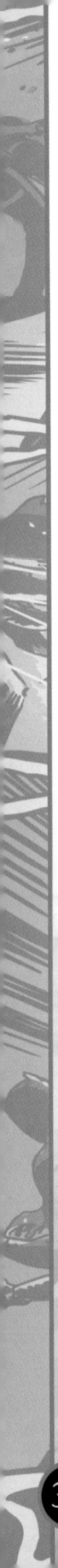

Erik Killmonger

The villain Erik Killmonger is from Wakanda. He is one of Black Panther's greatest enemies. Killmonger challenges Black Panther to a fight. He wants to take Black Panther's throne and rule Wakanda! Can he be stopped?

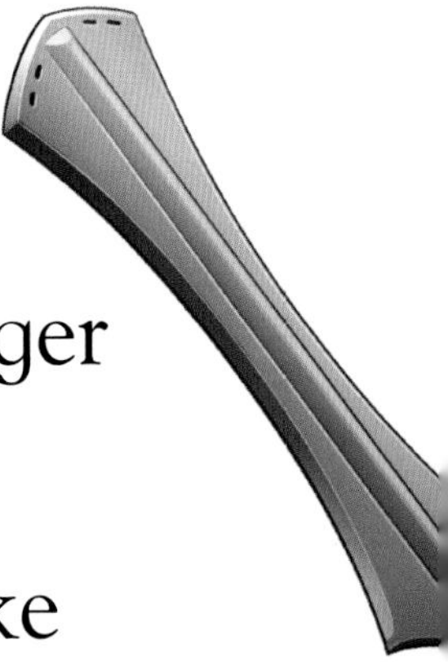

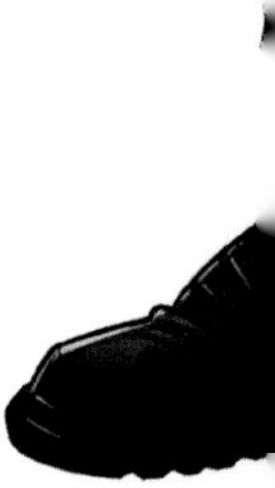

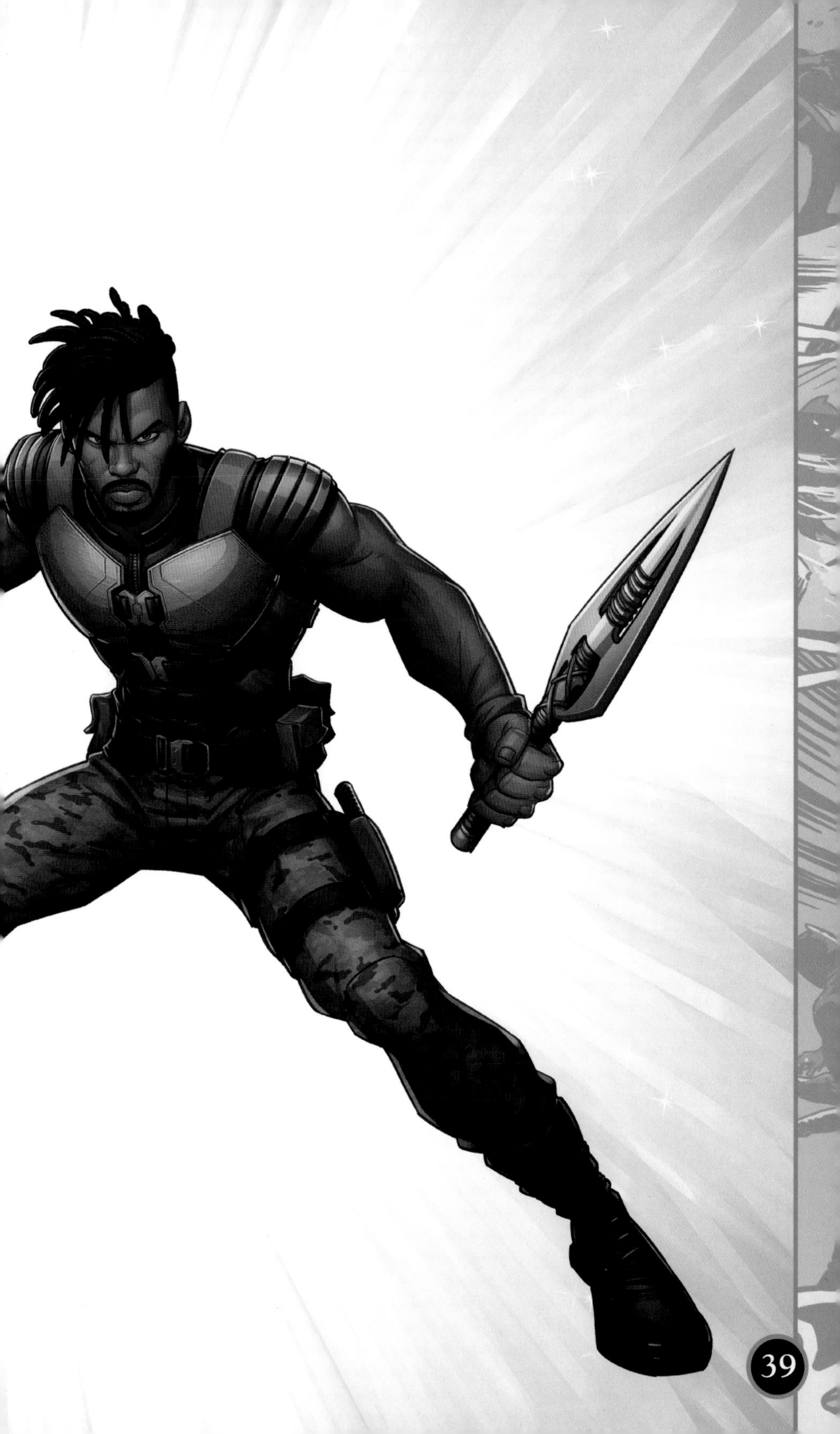

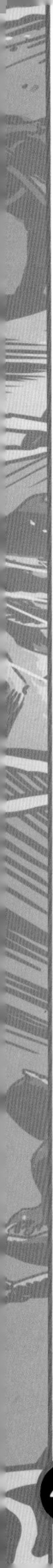

Ulysses Klaw

Ulysses Klaw is an evil villain and an expert in Vibranium. He hates Black Panther and has attacked Wakanda many times over the years! Just like Killmonger, he wants to rule Wakanda and control all of its technology.

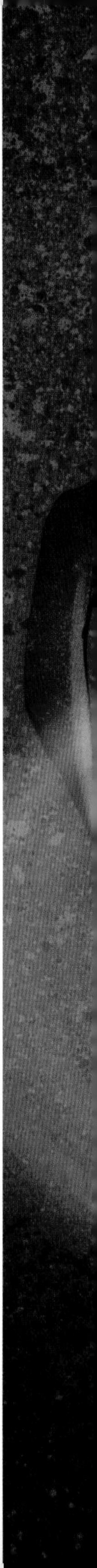

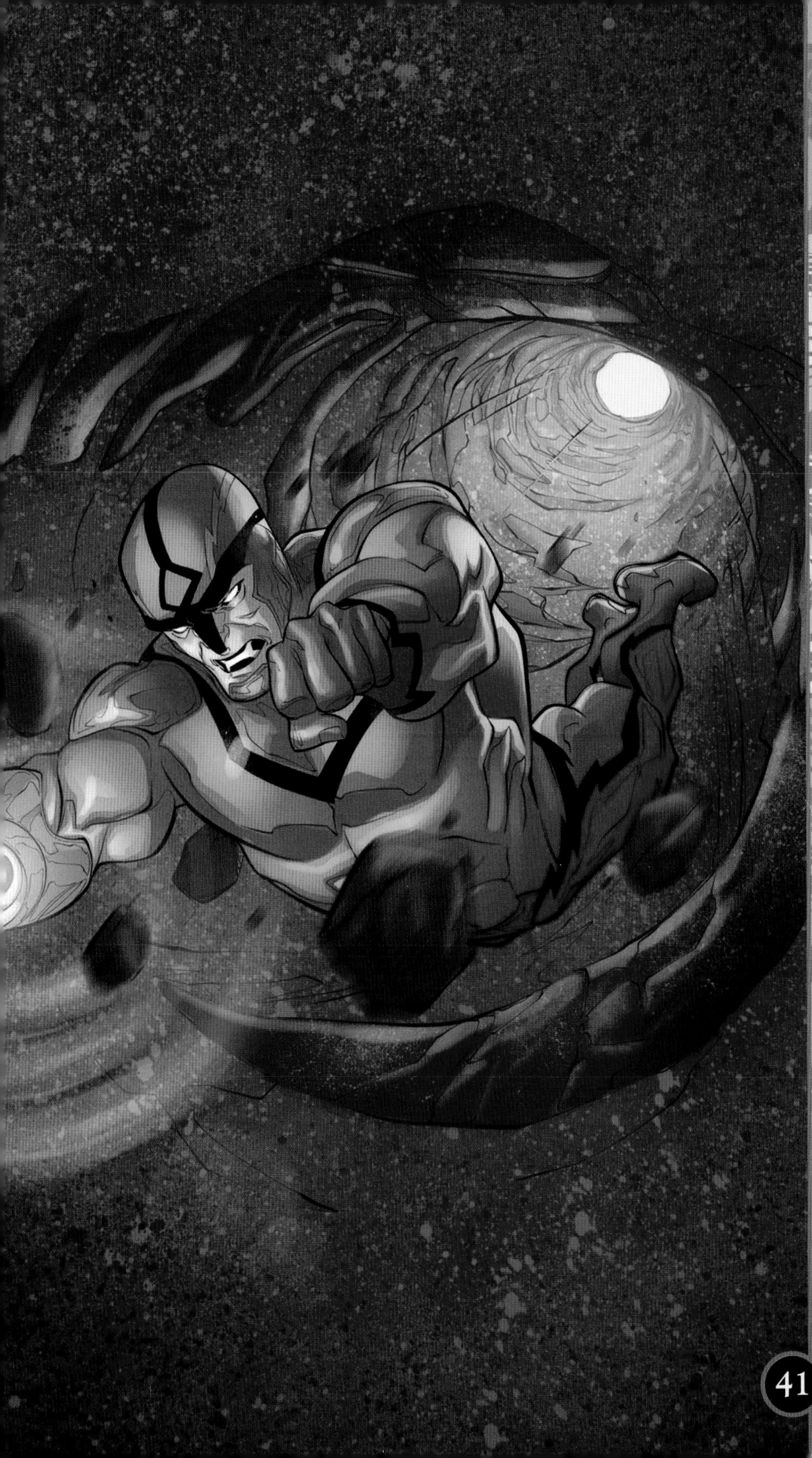

Wakanda forever!

When Shuri, Okoye, and Black Panther work together, they are very hard to beat.

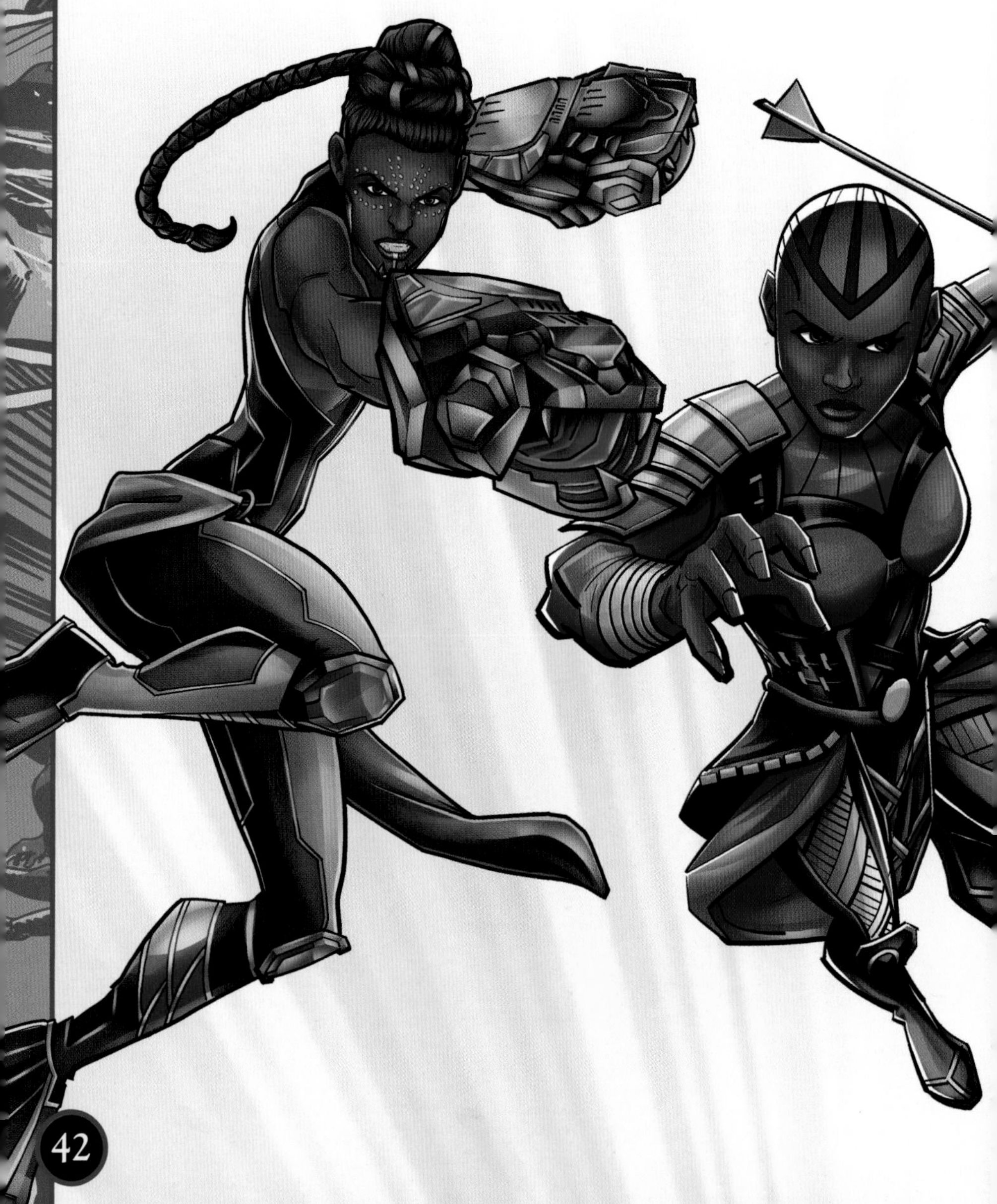

Whenever Wakanda is under attack, Black Panther and his team will bravely defend their home. Wakanda forever!

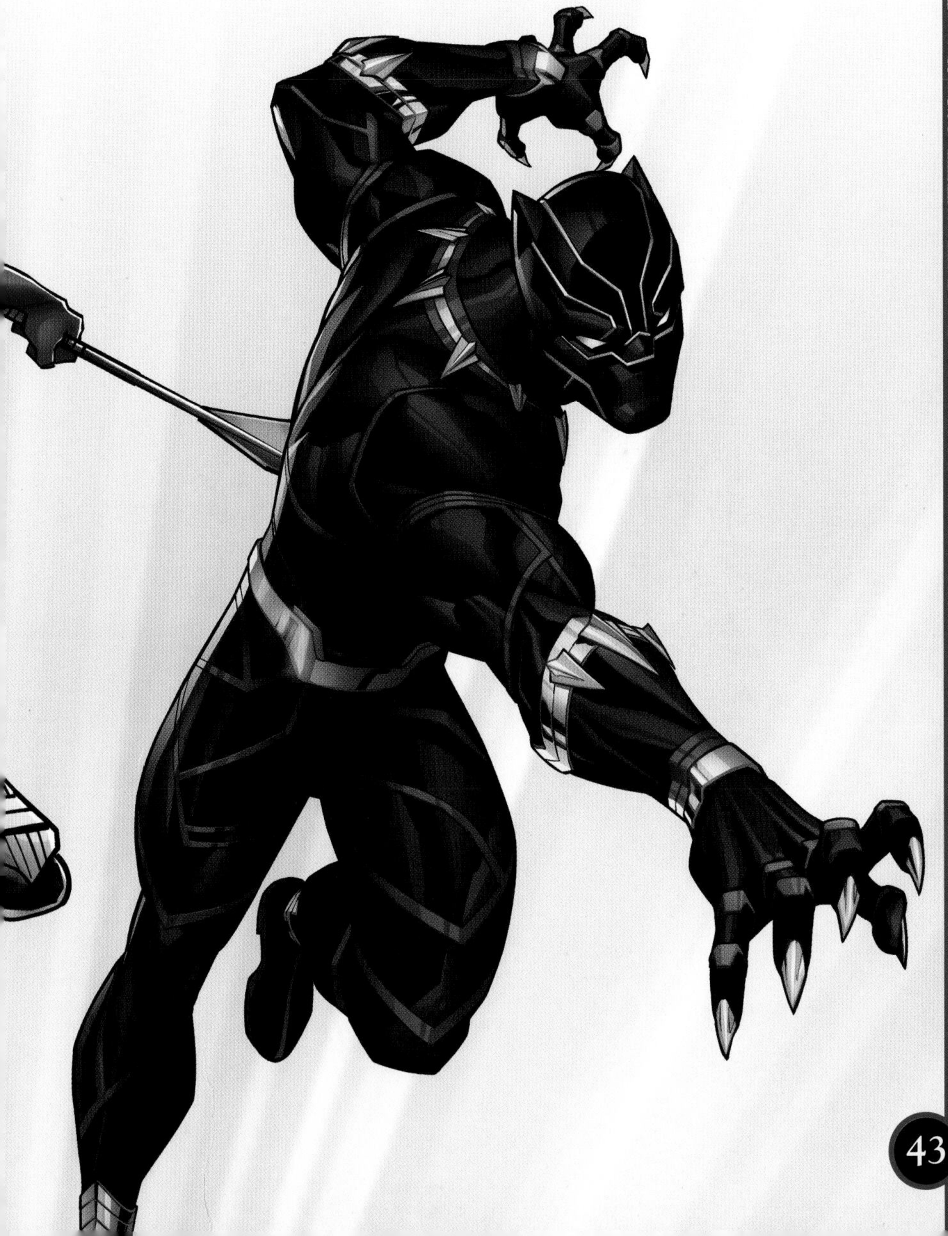

Quiz

1. What rare metal do Wakandans use in their technology?

2. Which villain is from Wakanda?

3. Who leads the Avengers?

4. Has Shuri been the Black Panther?

5. What is the name of Black Panther's suit?

6. True or false? Black Panther can call upon previous Black Panthers for help.

7. What weapon does Okoye use in battle?

8. Where is Wakanda located?

9. Why does T'Challa reveal Wakanda to the world?

10. Where does Queen Mother Ramonda come from?

Answers on page 47

Glossary

bodyguard
someone who protects others from harm.

energized
something that is energized is powered with energy.

hologram
a three-dimensional picture created with light.

inventor
a person who has ideas for new items.

meteorite
a rock from space that has landed on earth.

potion
a magical drink that gives special powers.

technology
machines that help people with a task.

wealthy
to be wealthy is to have lots of money.

Index

Answers to the quiz on pages 44 and 45:
1. Vibranium 2. Erik Killmonger 3. Black Panther 4. Yes 5. A Panther Habit 6. True 7. A Vibranium spear 8. East Africa, near Lake Nyanza 9. To make the planet safer 10. South Africa

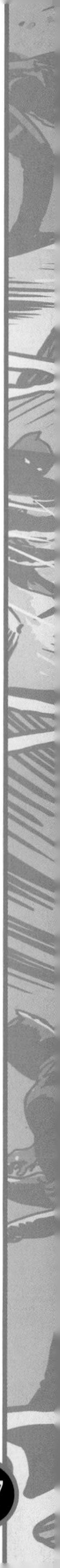

A LEVEL FOR EVERY READER

This book is a part of an exciting four-level reading series to support children in developing the habit of reading widely for both pleasure and information. Each book is designed to develop a child's reading skills, fluency, grammar awareness, and comprehension in order to build confidence and enjoyment when reading.

Ready for a Level 2 (Beginning to Read) book

A child should:

- be able to recognize a bank of common words quickly and be able to blend sounds together to make some words.

- be familiar with using beginner letter sounds and context clues to figure out unfamiliar words.

- sometimes correct his/her reading if it doesn't look right or make sense.

- be aware of the need for a slight pause at commas and a longer one at periods.

A valuable and shared reading experience

For many children, reading requires much effort, but adult participation can make reading both fun and easier. Here are a few tips on how to use this book with a young reader:

Check out the contents together:

- read about the book on the back cover and talk about the contents page to help heighten interest and expectation.

- discuss new or difficult words.

- chat about labels, annotations, and pictures.

Support the reader:

- give the book to the young reader to turn the pages.

- where necessary, encourage longer words to be broken into syllables, sound out each one, and then flow the syllables together; ask him/her to reread the sentence to check the meaning.

- encourage the reader to vary her/his voice as she/he reads; demonstrate how to do this if helpful.

Talk at the end of each book, or after every few pages:

- ask questions about the text and the meaning of the words used—this helps develop comprehension skills.

- read the quiz at the end of the book and encourage the reader to answer the questions, if necessary, by turning back to the relevant pages to find the answers.

Reading consultant: Dr. Barbara Marinak, Dean and Professor of Education at Mount St. Mary's University, Maryland.

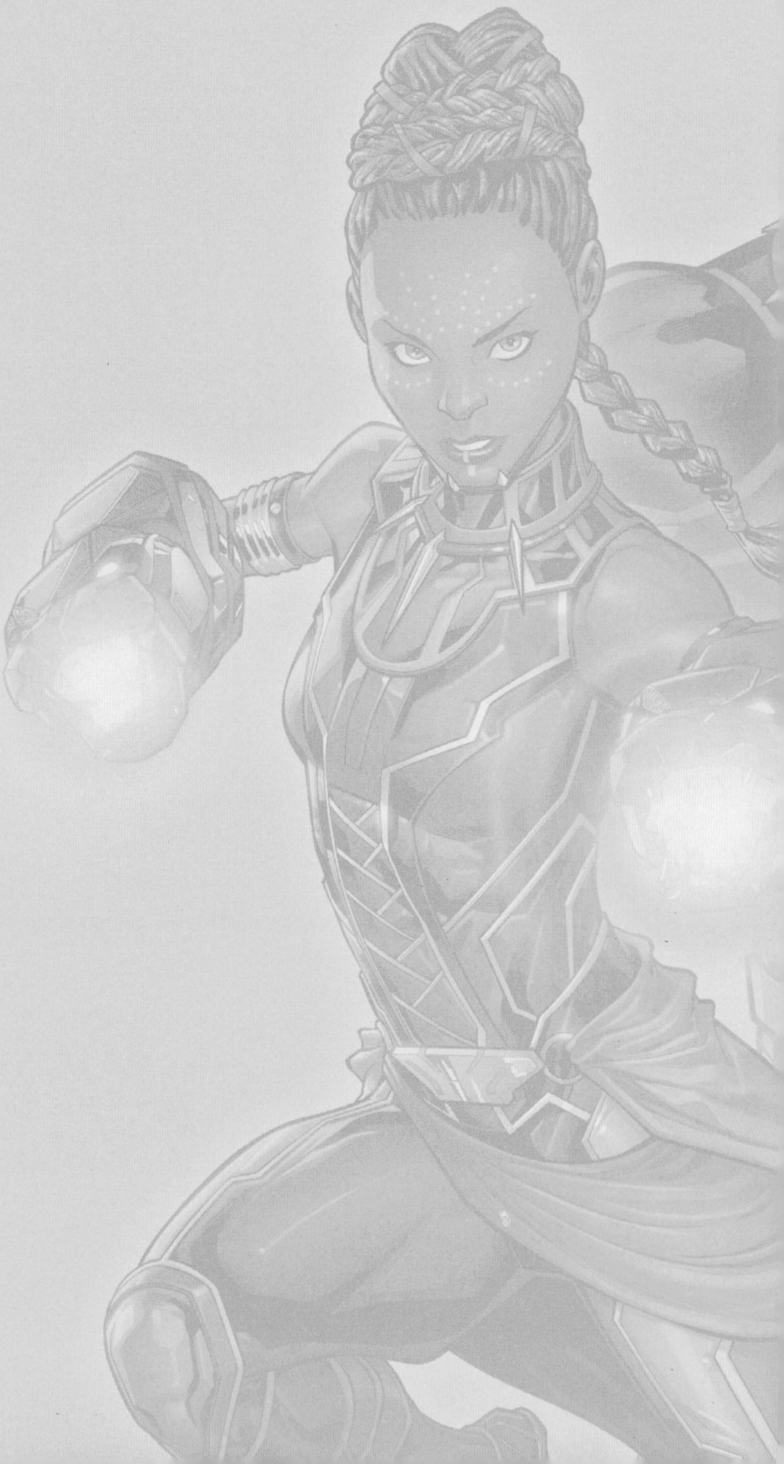